COWBOY'S CURVY NANNY

J.P. COMEAU

Copyright © 2020 by J.P. Comeau
All rights reserved.
No part of this book may be reproduced in any form or by any electronic or mechanical means, including information storage and retrieval systems, without written permission from the author, except for the use of brief quotations in a book review.

Cowboy's Curvy Nanny is a work of fiction. All names, characters, places, and occurrences are the product of the author's imagination. Any resemblance to a person, living or deceased, events, or locations is purely coincidental.

1

Bryce

I clicked my tongue. "Come on, Sky. That's a good girl. Come on. Got a nice sugar cube for you."

Sky shook out her mane as her head swayed from side to side.

"Come on, girl. We've been through this a million times. What in the world is--?"

A crash of thunder broke right above our heads, and Sky reared up onto her hind legs. I tossed the sugar cubes into her feeding trough before I rushed to her, gripping her swinging lead rope as I started to softly pat her side. And as lightning flashed across the sky, I turned my eyes to the heavens.

Hell of a day to have a storm.

I had been training Sky for barrel racing ever since she was a small foal. The runt of the family and a couple of hands beneath the rest of the horses I had, she always did have an attitude that couldn't be cooped up within her smaller-than-average body. But, today had been the worst of days, and I didn't need her reluctance to make it any worse.

Because if I couldn't get her into the trailer, I couldn't get her to the vet.

"Come on, sweet girl. We gotta get out of here. You want to jump at the thunder, or be soaked by the rain?"

Sky harrumphed and shook out her mane again. So, I petted down her side a bit more.

"I know you're scared. I know you hate storms. But, if you do this for me, there's a lovely treat in it for you. How's that sound?"

She slowly looked back at me, and it made me chuckle.

"I can't tell ya the treat, Sky. That ruins the surprise. But it's gonna be a good one. Whaddaya say?"

Her eyes narrowed before she finally took a step forward.

"There's my good girl. Here we go. Up and at 'em."

I got Sky loaded into the trailer as lightning continued to pierce across the heavens. A thunderous crack pumped blood through my veins, and I felt Sky trembling at my touch. It killed me to feel how scared she was, but I had rescheduled this vet visit twice already. Sky needed her yearly check-up, and I needed to make sure she was primped and primed for the barrel racing event at the local rodeo next weekend.

After hooking up Sky's lead rope so she would stay stable on the ride, I inched my way out of the stock trailer. I shielded my eyes from the pouring rain as it battered against my truck. When I heard Sky whinnying in the back, it broke my heart. I knew she wanted to be in the comfort of her stall, but we had one more stop we had to make. I hopped behind the wheel of the truck and cranked the engine.

Glancing in my rearview mirror, I gave the Rocking R Ranch's practice arena one last look and headed toward the main entrance to the Remington family's ranch.

As I drove slowly along the dirt road toward Dr. Morris' office, I sighed. I wondered what else was in store for me with this horrific day I'd been having. I mean, just this morning, I'd spilled hot coffee on myself and had to change. Twice. Not to mention, the only thing I'd had to eat was a chili dog at ten in the morning. So, I was starving, yet somehow overcome with heartburn at the same time. I could hear my wife's voice in my head now once I got home and started sucking down Tums.

You know your body can't handle that stuff anymore, Bryce.

I pushed the thoughts of my wife away, so I wouldn't have to even think about our altercation this morning. At the beginning of our relationship, all I had to do was mention a rodeo, and she was there. But, here lately, it was like pulling teeth to get her to come. She hadn't been to the last three rodeos, and with her absence came the absence of my daughter, Marie Lee. My two-year-old little starlight loved the rodeos, and every time her mother said she couldn't come, I had to leave the house listening to her squeals and cries of disapproval. It broke my heart. And I had no idea why the hell Patricia wouldn't just let me take her while she stayed behind. I mean, I fed her the argument any way I could. She'd get some alone time. She could go to whatever she wanted while I took care of Marie Lee. She could have herself a spa day, and I'd take care of everything once I got home. Nothing I suggested worked, though.

It was as if my wife didn't want Marie Lee to come with me out of spite.

And I couldn't understand why.

Something else is going on with her. Or, someone else?

I shook the thought away from my brain. Just because my wife didn't want to come to rodeos anymore didn't mean she was seeing someone else. Because if there was one thing the two of us had in common, it was our dedication to one another. We got together under less-than-ideal circumstances, and somehow we'd managed to make it work with a child involved. That took guts and a great deal of risk. I'd always admire her for that, too. No, no, there had to be something else. And once I could pinpoint what it was, I could take on the task of repairing what I knew was damaged between us.

After all, rodeos had been my favorite part of growing up. All of my best memories had been from the rodeos I attended with Mom and Dad and my two brothers. And I wanted my daughter to have those memories, too.

As I steered from the dirt road onto the paved driveway and approached my sprawling ranch house, I pushed all thoughts from my mind. One thing at a time is what I needed, so that's what I'd do. Once I got to the other side of town, and through this vet appointment, I could come back home and talk with Patricia. We always did our best talking over a milkshake after dinner once Marie Lee got put to bed, and we needed a really good talk now. I felt more distanced from her than ever before.

But, as I drove past my house, I made the mistake of slowing down to survey my lawn.

And I saw Marie Lee pressed against one of the front windows with tears pouring down her cheeks.

"That's enough," I murmured.

I rolled past the house slowly as I dug my cell phone out of my pocket and promptly called Patricia.

"Yeah?" she asked.

I heard Marie Lee wailing in the background, and it clenched my gut with anger.

"Why the hell is our daughter still at the window crying?"

She sighed. "She's been going back and forth from that window since you left. I think she's waiting for you to get home."

My heart seized in my chest. "Let me take her to this vet appointment. She can sit with me in--."

She huffed. "Why in the world do you always assume I can't handle our daughter?"

"Patricia, it isn't anything like that."

"Well, every time this girl is upset, you look to me to accuse me of something. I can hear it in your voice right now. Look, she's fine. She's not bleeding. She's not dying. She's just upset that she's not with you. She can hang on until you get home."

"Why won't you just let me take her to the vet? What's wrong with that?"

She clicked her tongue. "Look, I have to go. You're going to ruin our dinner tonight if you keep me on the phone any longer. See you when you get home."

"Patricia, wait. Give Marie Lee kisses for--!"

She hung up on me, and for some reason, I wasn't having it. So, I looked down at my screen as I eased to a stop and called her right back. I sat at the stop sign with my hazard lights on, letting anyone who needed to go around me do as such. And as the phone rang in my ear, Patricia finally picked up.

"Seriously. This entire dish is time sensi--."

"It's ten in the morning, Patricia. Your roast will be fine. I want to know why you won't try to calm down our daughter."

She paused. "Seriously?"

"Yes. Seriously."

I heard something clatter in the background. "Fine. All right. I won't calm her down because you spoil her. She's becoming nothing but a brat that demands things when she wants it and then throws herself onto the floor when she doesn't get it. You think every time you leave, this house is the only time she cries? I had a knock-down, drag-out fight with a two-year-old over chocolate for breakfast that resulted in her being put in her bed until she calmed down. You want to know how long that took?"

I shook my head. "There has to be another way to do this."

I heard venom rising in her voice. "That's fine if you want to think I'm a shit mother, but I know damn well and good what I'm doing. While you're in an office or out rodeoing twenty-four-seven, I'm here at home taking care of our daughter. Doing research. Talking with other moms about what works for *their* kids. And then you get me on the phone after only seeing your daughter for a few minutes this morning--."

"I told you to let me take her with me. And why are you cooking dinner anyway? Where the hell is Maria? The entire reason why we hired Maria was because you felt overwhelmed with motherhood and all of its responsibilities. Remember?"

"In this rain, Bryce?! Are you crazy!? She'd get sick! I told you the heavens were gonna open up today and to stay home and just not go, but you refused. You didn't want to do it. Because after working sixty hours in an office or training, you spend your entire weekends at the damn rodeo instead of here with your family. So, as far as I'm concerned? Until you spend more than ten hours a week with your daughter, you don't get a say in how she's raised."

She took a deep breath before she continued. "And by the way? Cooking soothes me. Can't have two girls crying and yelling up a storm in the same house."

I felt my anger boiling over. "You listen here, Patricia. I'm just as much of a parent as--."

She giggled bitterly. "Save your diatribe for some other father who's never home. But, right now? I've got dinner to prepare and a girl to raise. So, I'll talk to you whenever it is you get home. If I'm still awake by the time you get home."

And yet again, she hung up the phone on me. Leaving me sitting there at the stop sign, wondering if her words were true.

Am I a bad father?

Am I an absent father?

Is the solution to all of this simply giving up barrel racing?

I cursed beneath my breath and tossed my cell phone into the passenger seat of the truck. I didn't have time to weight the truth and the falsities of our fourth fight this week. I had to get to the vet before Dr. Morris canceled on me again and sent me across town to another vet's office that charged me twice as much for the same services.

So, I eased through the stop sign and continued on my way with the sounds of my crying daughter echoing off the corners of my mind.

2

Willow

Thunder cracked outside Dr. Morris' window as I sat there, my leg crossed over my knee. I'd always felt comfortable in his office. But, then again, I'd spent a lot of time in here as well. I grinned at the memories we'd created in the place. The memories his desk held. The memories his wall held. The memories his carpeting held. I watched as Dr. Morris' fingers flew across his keyboard. Long, dexterous, nimble fingers that made me shiver from head to toe. I ran my eyes along the parts of him I could see. The sleek blonde hair that contrasted his brooding brown eyes. The sun kissed skin that boasted of the time he spent in the sun and whisking me away to beaches that held even more fond memories.

I squeezed my thighs together in anticipation of our next encounter.

But, when Dr. Morris finally looked over at me, the expression behind his eyes gave me pause.

"Is... something wrong?" I asked.

He clasped his hands together and settled them on his desk before his eyes roamed my body. A smile slid across my face as I puffed my chest out with pride. A chest that had grown these past couple of weeks and forced me to go up half a bra size. Sure, I'd been eating a bit more than usual. But, it was Dr. Morris' fault. He kept taking me out to these amazing restaurants for dinner that used way too much butter in their food, and I always walked away with leftovers. Sure, maybe I'd put on ten pounds or so. But, who cared?

Especially since Dr. Morris kept raking his eyes over--.

"This isn't easy for me to say," he finally spat out.

My chest deflated. "What isn't easy for you to say?"

Thunder crashed outside again as he leaned back into his leather chair. The expression behind his eyes was one of concern and hesitation. I knew that look, though. This was the look of a man who was about to break things off with me. I swallowed hard as the smell of disinfectant wafted up my nostrils. The bright and peaceful white of his office now became cold and hard. Unforgiving, as he sat there, staring at me.

"Brandon, just spit it out," I said flatly.

His eyes found mine. "I can't continue to let you barrel race my horses."

I furrowed my brow. "What?"

He shook his head. "I'm sorry, Willow. But, I can't allow you to barrel race my horses anymore."

Is that it? "I mean, I have to say I'm a bit relieved."

He blinked. "Relieved?"

I nodded. "Yeah. For a second there, I thought you were about to break up with me."

He leaned forward. "Willow..."

My jaw hit the floor. "Holy shit, you *are* breaking up with me."

"Willow, listen to me."

I shot to my feet. "I've spent six months with you, sneaking around in the shadows and meeting you in the backs of restaurants to keep us out of view because I'm your employee, and you were worried about how that looked. And I was totally okay with that, right?"

He slowly stood. "Keep your voice down, Willow."

"Oh, like this!?"

My words echoed off the hardened corners of his office as his stare turned to a glare.

"This isn't easy for me to say. I've been trying to come up with the words for days," he said.

I scoffed. "Days?"

"Yes."

"Days."

He sighed. "Willow, please."

I took a step toward his desk. "Exactly how many days are we talking? Because if we're just talking the last two or three days, then you have to understand that we've had a date and three separate intimate outings in the last two or three days, Brandon. So, how many days *exactly* have you been fucking me and not telling me you wanted to break up?"

His back straightened. "Fine. If you're going to cause a scene, I'll spit it out and be done with it. I can't let you barrel race the horses anymore because you've put on a bit of weight, and it's too much of a strain on my horse's joints. You know a barrel racer has to keep their weight in check. You've been doing this your entire life, or so you've told me. But, every time I see you, things are a little…"

"Bigger? Thicker? Please, don't stop now on my account."

His eyes narrowed. "And I knew the second I threw all of this out onto the table for the sake of my horses, you'd take it personally. I like your curves, Willow. They're amazing. But, they aren't fit for racing horses. That's just a practical fact."

"So, you breaking up with me is simply a courtesy call?"

He shook his head. "It's not like that. I just wanted to--."

I pointed at him. "You know, my friends never did like you. Sadie and Luna? They both warned me about you. They both told me you'd do this. That you'd never actually take our relationship public and deal with the ridicule of dating one of your employees. I thought you cared about me, Brandon. Was any of it ever real?"

As he stared at me with his lips rolled over his teeth, the shockwave of insanity barreled over my body. I heard my best friend's voices in my head now, chanting away at the mantras that had practically become our only form of conversation when it came to the topic of Brandon.

He's just keeping you around because you're a champion barrel racer.

He's not going to have a public relationship with you.

Can't you see he's just screwing around with you because you're convenient?

You deserve better.

You know the rumors around town. You know he does this to all of his female hires.

"It wasn't real, was it?" I asked softly.

Dr. Morris came from around his desk. "I want you to listen to me, okay?"

I stepped away from him. "Don't you dare touch me."

"Trust me, I wasn't going to try."

I shook my head as I turned my back to him. "God, I'm such an idiot."

"You're not an idiot, Willow. You're one of the smartest women I've ever been with."

Been with. Not dated. "You never had any plans to date me, did you?"

"What do you think all of those dinners were?"

I slowly turned to face him again. "You mean, the dinners in the backs of those restaurants? You mean, dinner we sometimes got to-go, so we wouldn't be seen in public? You mean those dinners?"

"I thought you understood my predicament."

My voice fell flat. "I understand now that a man will say anything to fuck a woman he wants."

His voice grew hard. "Now listen, I won't have someone on my team addressing me in this manner. Now, I've said my piece. I can't let you race the horses anymore because of your weight gain. It's nothing against you, it's just business. And if you're going to allow that to affect what we've got going here--what *you've* got going here--then that's on you. Not me."

I narrowed my eyes. "Did you just threaten my job over this?"

He shrugged. "At the end of the day, you're still my employee. And we're having this conversation on company time. Take that for what it's worth."

I'd had enough. "You know, I brought a lot of attention and notoriety to your side hustle of barrel racing."

He nodded. "And I'll always be indebted to you for it. Just remember the NDA you signed."

"Yeah, yeah, yeah. Can't talk about your trade secrets with the competition. I got it."

"Or our relationship."

I paused. "Come again?"

He opened one of his desk drawers. "In your contract, it states that you can't talk about trade secrets. You can't disclose the condition of my horses or how they're trained, and you can't talk about any intimate details of myself to the competition. That includes our relationship."

I watched him pull out the contract before he handed it to me. But, I felt too blindsided to take it.

"You--wrote our relationship into that contract?" I asked breathlessly.

"Just intimate details. I didn't know how intimate things would really get."

"And yet you failed to disclose this to me?"

He tossed the contract onto his desk. "Didn't you read it? It's right there on the front page."

"I can't believe--!"

I closed my eyes and drew in a long breath as I tried to calm my quaking nerves. I felt so used. So abandoned. So--so angry. I'd never felt fury like this before, and it as rushed through my veins, I heard Sadie's voice echoing off the corners of my mind.

One day, I hope you stick it to that asshole. And not in a sexy way, either.

So, with a renewed sense of vigor, I opened my eyes and forced a calm expression over my face.

"Dr. Morris?"

His head fell off to the side. "Yes, Miss Jackson?"

"You're seeing someone else, aren't you?"

He snickered. "You really think that's what this is about?"

I shook my head slowly. "No. But, I do think your changed demeanor with me the past few weeks lends itself to having someone else on the side. Is it true?"

"What changed demeanor?"

"You know what I mean. Our nightly conversations stopped. Our playful demeanor in work stopped. And while you might be able to chalk the second one up to appearances, you can't do that with the first one. What happened to those conversations of ours? Did you transfer them to someone else? Did you start seeing someone on the nights we weren't together?"

He sat back down. "You can accuse me of all you want, Miss Jackson. But, the truth of the matter is that things between us have been suffering for a long time. You kept pressuring me into a public relationship I wasn't ready for--."

"You said at the beginning that's what we were working for!"

He shot back up to his feet. "Calm your voice, or you're fired."

I slowly walked up to his desk and placed my hands against the edge. I forced my tits together, giving him one last look at the luscious pillows he'd never lean his head against again. I looked up at him from beneath my thick, curled eyelashes and really poked my ass out there. Then, I lowered my voice to that tone I knew shivered him from head to toe.

"No need to fire me, Dr. Morris."

He swallowed hard. "You know what that voice does to me."

I winked up at him. "Because I quit, sweet cheeks."

His face fell. "What?"

I raised up slowly. "I. Quit."

"Willow, you don't have to leave your job. I just can't have you--."

"I quit, Brandon! I quit, I quit, I! Quit!"

I roared the words and listened to them echo off the walls.

I took pleasure in how Brandon winced at the volume of my voice. I turned on the heels of my boots and marched my way out of his office, throwing the door wide open. And as other vet techs and the front desk girl poked their heads out into the hallway, I noticed something.

They're all women.

"Have fun with him, girls! I'm outta here," I said.

I marched down the hallway and forced my way into the lounge. I walked over to my locker and slid my things out, sliding my purse over my shoulder. Thunder rumbled off in the distance as lightning flashed through the windows, illuminating the cheese danishes someone had brought in for breakfast.

"Takes a lot of calories to keep up these curves," I murmured.

So, instead of grabbing one, I grabbed two.

Suck on that, Doctor Douche.

I shoved one into my mouth as my purse fell to the floor. I slid into my raincoat before picking my purse up, then wrapped the second cheese danish in some napkins. I set it gingerly in my purse before finishing my massive bite of the other danish, and I felt all eyes on me as I turned toward the door.

A few of the girls stood in the entryway, watching me as I scarfed down that danish.

And I did it in style, licking up every ounce of sugar left behind on my lips and my fingertips.

"Mm, mm, mm! That's good stuff, right there," I said.

Dr. Morris' voice piped up from behind the girls. "If you want to get back to barrel racing, maybe you should try carrots instead."

I shot back without even thinking. "And if you want to keep dating women in your office, I suggest you stop pissing off the ones you've already slept with."

The girls gasped as I pushed through them in the doorway. I knocked my shoulder against Brandon's as I headed for the front doors, ready to blow this popsicle stand. I didn't care if he slapped me with a lawsuit. If he really tried to come after me for breaking some bullshit NDA. He could do whatever he wanted, but I'd never let that sorry excuse for a man touch me again. Literally, or metaphorically.

"You shouldn't have done that, Miss Jackson!"

His voice ricocheted down the hallway after me as I paused. For a brief second, I thought he was threatening me. Then, I decided I didn't care. I peered over my shoulder with a smoldering look in my eye, hellbent on making his life a living nightmare.

"If you take me to court, Dr. Morris, then nothing is stopping me from telling an entire courtroom full of people that you suck your thumb while I'm sucking your--."

His face grew red. "Enough!"

I smiled. "Oh, Brandon. You can kiss every single dimple that lines my ass crack."

I shoved my way out the front door, and I could've sworn I heard someone clapping their hands behind me. Almost as if they were cheering me on. I held my head high as I rushed down the ramp, trying to evade the pouring rain as much as possible. But, as soon as my feet touched the asphalt of the parking lot, I ran into something sturdy.

Something large.

Something unwavering, as I felt myself falling to the ground.

"Shit!" I exclaimed.

"Whoa, whoa, whoa. Hold on there."

A strong hand wrapped itself around my waist and pulled me back to my feet as if I weighed nothing. I felt myself grow breathless as rain battered down against my face. With my wet hair dripping down my cheeks and my coat completely soaked, I gazed into the face of my small-time hero.

And found a familiar pair of baby blues staring back at me.

"Bryce?"

His arm dropped from my waist. "Willow? You okay?"

I peered behind him. "Bringing in Sky again?"

He looked over his shoulder. "Yeah. Still got that thing with her hip. Can't figure it out for the life of me."

"Poor thing. I hope you get it worked out."

His eyes found mine again, and their stoic nature robbed me of my breath again. "You good?"

I swallowed hard. "Yeah, yeah. I'm good."

"You sure?"

"Yep."

"Kinda came out of there like a bat outta hell."

I giggled bitterly. "Yeah, well. Consider it my last stand."

He quirked an eyebrow. "Last stand?"

Thunder cracked again, causing me to jump. "I need to get out of this rain. Good luck with your appointment."

He nodded. "Thank ya, ma'am. Hope things get better for you today."

Yeah. Me, too.

3

Bryce

Despite the fact that our conversation had died down, she didn't move. I figured she'd try to walk around me, or even run to get out of this rain. But, Willow just kept standing there, looking up at me as if she were waiting for something. And while I was soaked to the bone, my mama raised me to never leave a woman in a state of duress.

It didn't matter what shit had gone on in my marriage.

She'd be disappointed if you did it to two women in one day.

"You sure nothing's wrong?" I asked.

Willow blinked rapidly as if I'd pulled her from a trance. "Yeah, yeah. I'm good."

"Wanna give that one more go?"

She shrugged. "I mean, all men are pricks. But other than that, I'm good."

"All men are... pricks?"

"Yep."

"All of them?"

Her eyes met mine. "Every single one of them."

I nodded slowly. "Well, I hope you find someone who knows how to treat you better."

She snickered. "Find me a good Texas boy who's single and ready to mingle, and I'll show you a woman ready to give it one more try."

"Then, you need a good Texas man, Willow. Not a boy."

Her eyes danced between mine. "Maybe you're right."

I wanted to keep questioning her. I wanted to dig out the real reason she was upset. I mean, she couldn't be upset at me, right? That statement wasn't directed at me, surely. Because if we really wanted to talk semantics, she was the one that wasn't looking and ran into me. So, technically, all girls are pricks.

Nah, something else is going on.

Water was dripping off the brim of my Stetson as I stood outside with Willow, but I didn't care. She'd always been such a calming presence in Dr. Morris' office and seemed to have this special touch with animals. She was a gifted vet tech, and I was hoping she'd be present for Sky's appointment. But, by the look of her coat and her soaked-through purse, I figured she was going home.

Wait, she didn't get fired, did she?

"Well, anyway. I have to go. Got a danish in my purse that's probably soggy from the rain at this point."

I blinked. "You have a what?"

She pushed past me. "Have a good appointment, Mr. Remington."

I whipped around, looking after her. "Since when are we on a last name basis again?"

She turned around, walking backward. "Since you're married and it's not professional."

She had a point. "Well, if you need anything--."

"Goodbye, Mr. Remington!"

Her words had a harsh tone to them, so I didn't snap back. I simply watched as she got into her truck and drove off. I mean, my clothes were already drenched. My jeans felt twenty pounds heavier, and my boots were filled with water. What were another few minutes if it made sure Willow didn't crash into something as she peeled out of the parking lot? Whatever had her worked up, though, she wasn't happy at all.

And I wondered if Dr. Morris had pissed her off in some way.

Sky's whinnying from the trailer pulled me from my trance, and I quickly made my way inside. The rain finally seemed to be letting up, but the thunder was louder than ever. As far as my eye could see, there was nothing but dark clouds. Dark clouds that loomed over the whole of Conroe, as if threatening to swallow us all whole for our sins. I felt a shiver work its way up my spine. Something was in the air that I didn't like. Something big, though I couldn't suss out what it might be.

Then, the door behind me opened up.

"Mr. Remington!? Aren't you going to come inside?" Dr. Morris asked.

I turned to face him. "Yeah. Sorry."

He held the door open for me. "Brenda!"

The front desk woman stood. "Yes, sir?"

Dr. Morris looked me up and down. "Get this man a few towels to dry off with. And something warm to drink."

Brenda disappeared. "Right away, sir."

I shook my head. "That isn't necessary."

Dr. Morris looked me over. "Sky still in the trailer?"

I took the towels Brenda brought for me. "Thanks. And yes, she is."

"All right. I'll go out and get her around back. The hip still acting up?"

I looked over at him as I dried off. "Yeah, we were doing our morning workout at the ranch. I noticed it was worse after about five minutes."

Brenda's voice rose up beside me. "Hot tea, or hot apple cider?"

I looked over at her. "I'm fine, really. Bad day to forget my rain slicker."

Dr. Morris talked over me. "Hot cider, for both of us. Come with me, Mr. Remington. We'll get Sky set up, and you can watch."

Something felt off about his interactions. Sure, a lot of people rolled out the red carpet for the Remington boys. But, that's because we inherited our parent's massive petroleum company when Dad retired a few years back. People always made sure to go above and beyond in order to get in our favor, and while one of my brothers, Will, loved it, I wasn't a fan. That's why I came to Dr. Morris' vet clinic because he treated me like just another client.

...Until now.

Is there a full moon comin' along or something?

During the entire vet appointment, though--as I soothed Sky so the doctor could work--I kept thinking about Willow. Not in that way, though she was a very pretty girl. But, her absence was prevalent. She always brought such a nice tone to the conversation at our appointments, even if I didn't talk back much. She made this place feel more like home instead of like a cold hospital for pets and stock animals.

Not only that, but she went above and beyond for patients. She had been so trusted here that some of the house calls Dr. Morris made on a regular basis, he assigned to her. Like one time, last spring, when Willow came to Rocking R Ranch for an emergency birth. One of my mares had gone into labor early and was clearly struggling. I called Dr. Morris in a panic, and fifteen minutes later, Willow showed up at the metallic gate of my ranch. I watched as she coaxed that mare into relaxing. I watched as she inserted her arms all the way up to her elbows in order to assist with the delivery. And I watched as she saved both the life of my mare and the life of that beautiful foal.

She was a talented young woman.

Not only that, though, but she was a talented barrel racer. She was my fiercest competition in the mixed events out there on the circuit during the weekends, and her technique was unlike anything I'd ever seen before. It was no wonder she was a champion at her craft, and her knowledge of horses showed that.

I didn't like that she wasn't at this appointment.

"Dr. Morris?"

He grunted as he crouched down to peek underneath Sky.

"I need to go make a phone call. I'll catch up with you in a second."

He nodded mindlessly. "We'll be here, Bryce."

I walked to the other end of the outdoor facility Dr. Morris had for his larger animal patients and pulled out my cell phone. I had to shake the water off the waterproof case, then I quickly dialed my brother Will's number. I needed to shake myself from this trance. I needed to talk with him about some things. But, most of all, I needed to know that someone else was having a weird day today because of this damn storm.

"Hello, hello, hello! To what do I owe the pleasure of this phone call from my big brother?"

I chuckled. "You're an idiot, you know that?"

"You say such wonderful things to me."

I rolled my eyes. "So, what's the morning report? I haven't heard from you yet, and it's making me nervous."

"Morning report? The morning report is that it's storming like a hurricane outside right now. You know there's no drilling on stormy days like this. Too much risk of a lightning strike."

"Right. So, where are we with financials?"

He paused. "You mean, has there been a difference between yesterday afternoon when we had this conversation and now?"

I sighed. "Will, give me something."

"The vet appointment isn't going well, is it?"

I looked over at Sky and noticed she winced the second Dr. Morris put pressure on the outside of her hip.

"Not really," I murmured.

"Dude, I'm really sorry. I know how much you love Sky. But, you might have to face the fact that she isn't a racing horse. Not with that bum hip. It was dislocated during birth. You don't recover from something like that."

"She's a strong mare with a lot of heart. Sky deserves every chance I can give her to race. You know she loves it, you've seen her out there."

He clicked his tongue. "Just make sure you know when enough is enough."

I pinched the bridge of my nose. "Right. Yeah."

"So, why do I take it that's not the only thing on your mind?"

"Are you having as shit of a day as I am?"

He chuckled. "Uh, oh. What's happened?"

"It'd be easier to tell you what hasn't happened."

He barked with laughter. "Hit me with it."

"I spilled coffee on myself twice, and I've burned my stomach because of it. Patricia still won't let me take Marie Lee to these damn things, Sky's back in the vet office, and every female with two or four legs that I have run into today, I've somehow made unhappy."

"Well, yikes."

"Yeah. Yikes."

He snickered. "You sure you're the reason they're upset?"

I shrugged. "I know Patricia's upset with me. I know Marie Lee feels like I'm leaving her behind. I don't know what the hell's wrong with Willow--."

"Who's Willow?"

I sighed. "This vet tech that ran into me at Morris' office. Apparently, all guys are pricks because she ran into me, or something like that."

He laughed heartily. "Look, I don't think it's all you. But, I'm telling you, this is why I don't date. I find a woman who needs a nice night, we enjoy one another's presence, and then we go our separate ways. Then, you don't have to get into all this squirrely emotional nonsense."

I blinked. "Why don't you just try to patch things up with Sadie. I know it's been a long time... And did you really just use my marital fights and my daily difficulties to justify why you're a manwhore?"

"Hey. I resent that comment. I enjoy women, and they

enjoy me. Why would I rob them of that to stick with just one gal? That doesn't seem very fair, does it? And besides, Sadie definitely still hates me."

"Says the guy who won't sleep with a girl if she's had multiple partners. How fair is that? The same guy who hasn't gotten over his high school squeeze."

"You're on the chopping block right now, not me. Remember that."

I chuckled bitterly. "Ugh, I need this day to be over."

He perked up. "That reminds me! Are we still meeting in the ring to practice at three? Or, does this vet appointment kind of eat into that plan?"

"It's only eleven-thirty."

"You know what I mean."

I looked over my shoulder at Sky again. "Yeah, we'll be there. I don't know what kind of condition Sky will be in, but she'll be happy to just have a space that's familiar to her after the chaos of today."

"Good. Because the rodeo next week is high stakes. And if Sky isn't going to race, we have to find a horse that can step up to the plate. Us Remington boys have a reputation to keep up, you know."

I grinned. "Looking forward to it."

"And the fridge at the practice arena is well-stocked with Coors to have once we finish."

I nodded. "So long as I'm back for dinner at seven, I'm good."

"Seven? Seriously? That cuts out two hours of--."

"I can come at two if it helps, but I have to be home by seven. All right?"

He sighed. "Fine, fine. We'll meet at two. But don't be late. We'll still be down a training hour this way."

I chuckled. "See you then, micromanager."

"See you then, lazy ass."

4

Bryce

Dr. Morris finally stood up. "All right, I think I figured out what's going on with Sky. LaShonda!"

A female voice piped up from the other end of the stalls. "Yes, Dr. Morris!?"

"Can you come here a second and help me?"

I heard the pitter-patter of footsteps before a beautiful black woman emerged. Her head held high, her back poised, and a wide smile on her face. She walked with the grace of royalty but wore clothes that denoted the fact that she took care of the animals back here that had to be kept overnight for recuperation or treatment. Her muddy jeans and her slobber-stained flannel shirt boasted of the hard work she did back here, and I wondered how long she'd been working for Dr. Morris.

I also found myself wondering if Dr. Morris employed anyone else other than beautiful women.

"Whatcha need, Dr. Morris?" the woman asked.

He thumbed over his shoulder. "I need that medicine cabinet for the horses out of the closet down there. I'm going to give Sky here something for the pain she's in and write up a script for something else."

The woman nodded. "Anything else?"

"When you get a chance, Markie needs to work on getting up on that leg. He's being a bit bullheaded about it."

She grinned. "He is a bull, Dr. Morris."

"And that's why I want you to do it. He seems to like you."

She shrugged. "Eh, you just gotta know how to treat them. That's all."

"Well, you do a marvelous job, LaShonda."

She smiled brightly, and said, "I appreciate the kind words," then turned to me, "I'll be right back. Mr. Remington."

I nodded. "Ma'am."

As I watched her walk off with all the confidence in the world, I couldn't help but let my mind run away from me. I mean, Willow had been with Dr. Morris for well over two years. And all of a sudden, she's fired? Everyone knew that this man went through female vet techs very quickly. I mean, a bunch of us were shocked when Willow stayed on as long as she did. But, with her being gone so suddenly--along with the longing way Dr. Morris stared after LaShonda--it made me wonder why Willow had actually been fired.

Was she one of the girls Morris had sacrificed to his appetite?

While it wasn't my place, I knew Willow deserved better. And that would've explained why a nice gal like her hadn't been seen with a nice guy or something for a while now. Again, none of my business, but I hated a womanizer. A man who used his position to get in good with women he hired just to get his dick wet. And if Dr. Morris really was that kind of man? Maybe I did need to stick to heading across town.

I'd gladly pay double the bill to support a man that wasn't a shithead.

"Here you go, Doctor," LaShonda said.

He nodded. "Thanks. Now, tend to Markie before he loses all control in that leg of his. He needs to stop being so stubborn and actually walk around on it."

She snickered. "You leave that to me. I'll make sure he's up and going before his owners come back next week."

I interjected. "Uh, Dr. Morris?"

He looked over at me. "Huh?"

"What is it you're about to give Sky?"

"Oh! Yes. This. It's a mild pain reliever. I do believe your lovely mare here is suffering from a few things, none of which are related. So, this will help with the discomfort until we can get arthroscopic surgery scheduled for this hip."

"Wait, wait, wait, wait. What else is going on?"

He slid the needle into Sky's skin. "Hold on there, girl. It's okay. Almost done.... And we're done! You did great, Sky."

I watched him pat her coat before he turned to face me.

"Well, she's constipated, for one. At first, I thought it was her stomach that was distended. But it's not. It's her bowels. Also, with that comes gas pains. I'm actually wondering if the gas that can't travel through her colon right now is what's making her hip act up; because her hip isn't even swollen right now. I mean, it does need surgery. But, she should've been able to perform just fine today without pain."

I blinked. "My mare's constipated?"

He chuckled. "Nothing a strong laxative won't fix. There's a good chance she's got a food allergy. To which I say: get her as all-natural of a food source as you can. Even if you have to grow your own crops. There's too much processed stuff in animal food these days. So, if you're preordering it? Make sure it's as natural as you can get. I know it'll cost more, but it'll keep stuff like this from occurring."

"Thanks, Doc. I owe you one."

He patted Sky again. "Nah, this is what I love to do."

Yeah. And women. "Still, I appreciate it. How long do you think it'll take the laxative to work?"

He shrugged. "Depends on the blockage. I'm going to prescribe a pretty strong one, but it's by no means the strongest. It should work well within 48 hours. But, you'll know quickly if it isn't working. If that happens? You call me, and we'll have to fix this girl manually."

I paused. "Right. Okay."

He chuckled. "Not as terrible as it sounds. And not as

painful, either. Sky will be more relieved once we're done than anything, all right? Nothing to worry about."

"When should we schedule this surgery you're talking about?"

He shrugged. "We can do it anytime. But, the next couple of weeks are very, very busy for me. If you want to get it in sooner than that, I can give Dale a call across town and see what his availability is."

"If it's not urgent, then we can wait until you're free again."

He nodded. "Fair enough. Let's go get you checked out so you can get Sky home."

LaShonda took control of Sky while Dr. Morris and myself headed back up to the main building. And when I met face to face with Brenda--his front desk woman--to schedule Sky another check-up, we couldn't find an open date.

"Oh, no. I'm so sorry, Mr. Remington. But, Dr. Morris will be at his Houston clinic on those days."

"I'm sorry, that doesn't work either. Conference week. He's supposed to be presenting all week in Vegas."

"It looks like Dr. Morris is going to be on vacation? I don't know, he's got it blocked off, but it doesn't specify why. He sometimes does that when he schedules his vacation time."

"Uh, that might work? I can put you down tentatively and give you a callback."

I sighed. "Boy, haven't had this much of a problem scheduling something since my own wedding."

She giggled. "We'll find you something, Mr. Remington. I promise."

I should have been able to shake the feeling, but there was something off about the whole interaction. It was the first time in well over a decade that I had actually been wait-listed with Dr. Morris' office. I mean, I'd heard of other people being wait-listed, but I had never been. And while I didn't like special treatment or anything, something seemed off about the whole transaction.

From the lack of time to see the doctor to the plastered-on smile, Brenda kept on her face.

This day has just been plain weird.

I shoved it from my mind, though, and headed on home. I drove the trailer up the dirt road that led straight to the stable I had on my sprawling property and quickly unloaded Sky. I had to run and pick up her prescription, but I wanted to take Marie Lee with me. I wanted my daughter to know that I hadn't abandoned her and if Patricia didn't like it? She could suck my nozzle. Not that she'd been doing anything like that for months now, anyway.

However, when I hopped back into my truck and headed down the main driveway, I noticed something odd.

"Where's Patricia's Range Rover?" I murmured to myself.

I heard Marie Lee kicking up a stink inside, so I leaped out of the truck. I didn't even bother keeping it running as I charged through the front door and followed the sound of my wailing daughter. I found her in the kitchen with Maria, who was trying to take over cooking up this damn roast my wife had been talking about while she held my daughter in her arms. And the second my daughter set her eyes on me, she reached out her hands.

"Da-da-daddy!" she screamed through her sobs.

Maria was more than relieved to hand her over to me as I cradled her.

"Hush little Marie, don't say a word. Daddy's gonna buy you a mockingbird."

I sang lowly to her as I rocked her in my arms. I felt her face lay against my shoulder as she continued to cry as helplessly as I'd ever heard. It broke my heart, and yet Patricia was nowhere to be found.

"Mr. Remington?" Maria asked.

I turned to face her. "You know you can just call me 'Bryce.'"

She pointed. "There. She left a note."

I furrowed my brow as I turned around and found what Maria had been pointing at. I walked over and picked up the note, scanning it with my eyes. And as I felt anger bubbling up the back of my throat, I pierced Maria with a jagged glare.

"Why the hell wasn't I called about any of this?" I asked.

"No phone!" Marie Lee screamed.

Maria pointed toward the bathroom, shaking her head. "My phone's ruined. It may as well be still in the toilet."

I bounced my daughter in my arms as I slammed the note onto the counter. But, the words already tumbled around in my head. As much as I wanted to forget them, the tears in my eyes told me I never would. And it made me sick to my stomach. Every time I tried to put my daughter down, she clung to me. Rightfully so, too. So, I walked into the living room and sat down on the couch as I continued singing softly to her.

"Hush little Marie, don't you cry. Daddy's gonna shade you from all the lies. And if those lies come back to hurt, Daddy's gonna punch them in the--."

"Sir?" Maria asked.

I sighed. "Bryce, Maria. It's Bryce."

"Want me to fix dessert with dinner?"

I snickered. "Might as well. At least something good will come of this day."

Marie Lee sniffled. "Is Mommy bye-bye?"

I felt her pick her head up, and when I gazed into the eyes of my two-year-old little girl, I didn't know what to tell her. All I heard in my head were the echoes of that fucking note Patricia dared to leave behind.

As much as this pains me to admit, I've found someone else, Bryce. I've told you for months now that money can't solve everything. You're a workaholic. You're never home to be the father you think you are, and I can't take it anymore. I already feel like a single parent, and I refuse to be married to that anymore. I'll contact you in a few days to check up on Marie Lee.

Goodbye, Bryce.

The entire thing made me sick to my stomach. I mean, I'd thrown my life away for the woman. I married her after we got pregnant to make sure someone made an honest woman out of her, especially in a small Texas town. I promised to give her everything simply because she was the mother of my child. And what did I get in return?

This.

I got an empty house, an even emptier ranch, and no one to help me run any of it.

I need a nanny.

And I needed a nanny quickly.

Willow

I picked up another slice of pizza and sympathized as Luna rattled on in my ear about her father's arthritis and how she was starting to help take care of him. I watched as darkness fell heavily over the Texas Hill Country, and I wondered if the darkness would do me the favor of swallowing me whole and never letting me go again. I knew the girls were going to give me a good tongue-lashing over how things ended between Dr. Morris and myself. Especially since they predicted it would happen a bit like this. But, I still needed to talk to them. Even through all of the 'I told you so's" that I resented from them, I knew they'd make me feel better after getting their jabs in.

Then, finally, Luna said something that caught my attention. "Do you think he's seeing someone else at your place of work?"

I blinked. "Well, I mean, I don't work there anymore. But, do you think he'd be that brazen?"

Sadie scoffed. "Are you kidding? The man's done worse, and you know it."

I sighed. "That's very true."

Luna paused. "What did you ever see in that man, anyway? I mean, he's balding a bit, isn't he?"

Sadie giggled. "And he's got that beer gut going nowadays."

Luna cackled. "And let's not forget those sandals with socks that he wore to the hoedown a few months back. The poor man looked like--."

I spoke with my mouth full. "All right, all right, all right. I get it. Dr. Morris isn't the most attractive man anymore. Yikes."

Sadie clicked her tongue. "Understatement of the year."

I grinned. "He sure had it going on in bed, though."

Luna whispered. "Ew."

Sadie paused. "I'm with 'Ew' over here."

I threw my head back with laughter. "Oh, come on, girls. Indulge me at least a little bit."

Sadie snickered. "Yeah, maybe. If Dr. Morris looked a bit more like Tom Hiddleston and a bit less like Dr. Phil."

My jaw hit the floor. "Sadie!"

She guffawed with laughter. "What?! I'm just saying!"

Then, Luna dropped in with a great idea. "What if we try to find out who this other woman is? You know, just to see who Dr. Morris has sucked into his web this time? No offense, Willow."

I blinked. "None... taken?"

Sadie clapped her hands. "Oh! Oh! That's such a good idea. I've got his Facebook page already pulled up."

I put my pizza down. "Wait, what?"

I heard Luna typing over the phone. "I've got his Twitter and his LinkedIn."

"Girls. I don't know if this is--."

Sadie sighed. "His Facebook is locked down pretty tightly. I sent him a friend request, but he probably won't pick it up."

I leaned back against the couch. "Probably not. I talked about you two a lot to him. He knows who you guys are."

Luna tsked. "Well, his Twitter and LinkedIn are blown wide open. And while his LinkedIn hasn't been updated in three or so years, there are some interesting pictures on his Twitter feed."

I blinked. "I don't have Twitter."

Sadie squealed. "I do! I do! I'm putting it up no--whoa."

I leaned forward quickly. "Whoa? What, whoa?"

"Yeah," Luna said.

"Hey! Guys! Tell me what the hell you're looking at!" I exclaimed.

Sadie sighed. "You remember when he couldn't go out with you a couple of weeks ago because he was apparently sick with the flu?"

I nodded. "Yeah?"

Luna cleared her throat. "Well, there is a slew of pictures

ranging from a week ago to two weeks ago with pictures of him in the Bahamas."

I stood up. "What?"

Sadie interjected. "On a yacht."

I blinked. "What!?"

Luna scoffed. "Cheering with champagne. And that other set of fingers is pretty dainty."

My vision dripped with red. "What!?!"

I flopped back down onto the couch and picked up another slice of pizza. I practically sucked it down before picking up another one while Sadie and Luna electronically stalked my ex. I tuned them out, though. I was so hurt and so blindsided by all of this that all I wanted to do was stare at a wall and eat my weight in cheesy goodness.

I'd never had a man leave me like this, much less cheat on me in the process.

The woman must really be a looker, then.

Sadie's voice ripped me from my trance. "All right, all right, I know this has been fun--."

I scoffed. "Speak for yourself."

Luna sighed. "We're sorry, Willow. But, now, at least you're seeing him for how we've always seen him. And maybe you'll listen to us next time when we warn you about guys like him."

I rolled my eyes. "Whatever."

Sadie interjected. "And anyway, you need to focus on finding another job. Not wallowing in this self-pity, you've got going for yourself. Because on my end? It doesn't look like the other vet in this town is hiring at the moment."

I paused. "You're now looking at jobs for me? What are you, the Wizard of the Internet?"

Luna jumped in. "She's right. The only full-time work I'm finding is at grocery stores and things like that. There's a lot of part-time work on the ranches around here and everything. But, still, nothing at the local vet clinics or even the ones in the surrounding towns."

Sadie piped up. "Hey, hey, hey! An idea just hit me. Oh, a good--very, very good--idea."

I took another bite of pizza. "What?"

"I ran into Will Remington at Beck's Bar across town when I went to get dinner, and--."

I grinned. "You sure you just willy-nilly ran into the man? Or, are you two finally talking again?"

The phone fell silent before Luna, and I started laughing. And Sadie wasn't a fan of it.

"Shut up, both of you. You know I still hate him."

I held my stomach as I leaned forward. "No you don't. You still have a crush on him."

Luna cackled with laughter. "Girl, he's definitely moved on. You made sure of that when you broke up with him."

Sadie murmured over the phone. "Why don't you shut up so I can talk about what he told me? I mean, Willow might like working for his brother."

My laughter stopped. "Wait, Bryce is looking for an employee?"

Luna settled her giggles. "Wow, you stopped laughing really quickly."

I heard Sadie's grin over the phone. "Any reason for that?"

My face fell. "The man's married, assholes. That's a really shitty thing to even consider. He's my friend, and nothing more. Is he okay? What does he need help with?"

Sadie paused. "Wait, you haven't heard?"

I slowly stood. "Heard what? Is Bryce all right?"

Sadie sighed. "I don't know the details, but the job assumes a lot about the position Bryce might be in."

Luna clicked her tongue. "Well? Spit it out, then."

I stood there, holding my breath before Sadie finally spoke again.

"Bryce needs a nanny to help with his daughter."

I let out the breath I'd been holding. "Where's Patricia in all of this? Did something happen to her?"

"I don't know. Will didn't go into all of that. But, the sadness in his eyes told me that whatever it is? It isn't good?"

Luna sighed. "Besides, word travels fast around this town. Everyone will know what happened by the weekend. So, we'll have our answers eventually."

I drew in a deep breath. "A nanny..."

The worst-case scenario ran through my mind, and I instantly wanted to give Bryce a massive hug. I mean, his wife always reminded me of some kind of gold digger, and it shocked the entire town when he proposed to that woman. They hadn't dated for long, if at all before they decided to get married. And while I believed in love at first sight, those two seemed completely incompatible with one another. I always wondered why a guy like Bryce would decide to build his family with a woman like that. But, if she had left him, maybe it was a good thing for him along down the road. That meant he could find a nice girl who'd treat him like a man instead of like a damn paycheck.

"I've always liked being around kids," I murmured.

"Exactly," Sadie said, "and since you know Bryce already, he might be more inclined to hire someone he knows to look after that precious little daughter of his."

Luna hopped in. "I say it's definitely worth a shot."

I weighed my options. "Think you girls can come up with his email for me?"

The phone call fell silent for less than thirty seconds before Sadie piped up.

"Got it!"

Luna cursed beneath her breath. "One click away."

I shook my head. "You two are insane, you know that?"

Sadie cleared her throat. "Ready? You want to write this down or remember it?"

I settled back against the couch cushions. "Send it to me in a text. I'm going to start crafting my email and updating my resume."

I heard clicking on the other end of the line before Sadie spoke up again. "Got it sent."

My phone lit up in my hand. "Thanks, girl. I appreciate it."

Luna giggled. "Let us know how it goes beautiful."

I nodded. "Will do."

"And if you need me to proofread anything, let me know, okay?" Sadie asked.

"Thanks. I love you guys."

"Love you, too," they said in unison.

Then, I started crafting my email and updating my resume, all on my phone. Hoping it would be enough to score a job I desperately needed, as well as fill a position that sounded almost like an emergency.

And who knows? Maybe Bryce would let me compete with the Remington's prized quarter horses in barrel racing events under his name. Kind of like I did with Dr. Morris. My reputation as a champion barrel racer would help bring attention to his hobby as a horse breeder. And it would keep extra money flowing in on the weekends for me.

"A win-win for everyone involved," I murmured to myself.

So, I included that little caveat in a 'P.S.' to the email. Just in case Bryce might be interested in that sort of a deal before I hit 'send'.

6

Bryce

Hello there, Bryce! It's Willow. Word around town says you're looking for a nanny. And it turns out, I'm looking for a job. I'm great with kids, and I did work with them professionally before I worked as a vet tech. I'm attaching my resume with this email, and I would forever be grateful if I could have an opportunity to interview for the position if you think I'm a good fit after reviewing my resume.

Willow

P.S.: I don't know if you're looking for another barrel racer or anything, but if you want, we could work something out there, too. Possibly a lower overall pay rate from nannying in exchange for me racing one of your *champion horses? Just think it over.* **It might be a win-win for both of us.**

As I sipped my morning coffee, I read over her email three or four different times. Not because I was shocked that word traveled beyond quickly in this insane little town, but because I wasn't sure why I hadn't considered Willow first. I mean, she'd be a perfect candidate for a nanny. She needed a job, I trusted her, I knew her--which was the best part of all this--and the idea of Willow with her championship title, racing our horses was tantalizing, to say the least.

Don't get ahead of yourself. At least look at her resume.

I downloaded the file onto my phone and watched it pop up. And when it fully rendered on my phone screen, my eyes bulged. The woman didn't just have experience with children, she had a degree in working in Early Childhood Education. I mean, this is what she went to school for!

I murmured to myself. "University of Houston graduated with a 3.4 GPA. Five certifications outside of school."

My eyes continued scanning her resume, and it seemed as if the vet tech job was the job out in left field. All of her other working experience from the time she graduated up until that job was working with children.

So, I quickly shot her back a reply to the email.

Willow,

I'd love to sit down and speak with you about the job. I'm going to put my number at the bottom of this email. Let's schedule a lunch meet-up so you can meet by daughter, Marie Lee, and we can see how you guys mesh.

B. Remington

I set my phone beside me and finished my second cup of coffee for the day. Then, my phone started ringing. I furrowed my brow as I looked down at the foreign number calling me, and it gave me pause.

It can't be.

But, when I picked up the phone? It was.

"Bryce?" Willow asked.

I chuckled. "I take it you sit by your phone like I do."

"When a job is on the line? Of course."

"You have a great deal of experience working with children. It shocked me, actually."

She giggled. "Yeah, well, the vet tech job with Dr. Morris was a great break away from the demand of those kinds of jobs. But I miss it. I miss kids running around. Animals just aren't the same, you know?"

"I can only imagine."

A pause fell over the phone before my mind jumpstarted itself again.

"All right. Well. Uh, what are you doing around twelve-thirty today? Do you have time to meet up for lunch?"

Willow snickered. "Got all the time in the world right now."

I grinned. "Right, right. Well, I'm free if you're free."

"I'm free this afternoon, yes. Got any place in mind where you want to meet?"

"To be honest? I'm not sure what's around here other than

the barbecue place up the road from my house. I'm either there, or grilling out back."

She groaned. "I haven't had a grilled at home meal in months. That sounds amazing."

"You want to just come here, then? I'll whip us up some lunch, and you can get a feel for how you'll interact with Marie Lee in a space she's familiar with."

"That sounds like it would be best for her, so I'm all for it."

I stood. "Great! Good! Well, uh, you know where I live?"

She giggled. "Well, yes. I came out for Dr. Morris, remember?"

"Oh, yes. Yes, of course."

"See you at twelve-thirty then, Bryce."

After hanging up the phone with Willow, I got to work on what to grill. I started preparing some burgers with my infamous dry rub. I stacked cheese cubes in the middle to give it a nice burst of a surprise that my brother loved. Then, I put them in the fridge to marinate. While Marie Lee tore up the house to keep herself entertained, I tried my best not to keep track of the mess, because I knew the second I started worrying about it, I'd stop to clean it.

Which meant lunch wouldn't be ready by the time Willow got here.

If I was being honest with myself? I'd probably hire Willow whether or not she and my daughter got along in the beginning. I knew Marie Lee would warm up to her like everyone else had when Willow moved into town a few years back. And doing things this way meant I didn't have to miss any more work. Even just taking off yesterday and today had already set me well behind schedule. I needed to get back into the office to play catch-up.

And especially with the business trip to Houston coming up soon.

Time flew by quickly, though, and just as I finished cleaning up, the doorbell rang. Marie Lee went rushing for the door, her unbalanced feet carrying her as quickly as she could. But, when she reached for the doorknob, I scolded her.

"Uh, uh, uh, Marie Lee."

She slowly looked up at me. "Wha?"

"We don't open doors without permission, right?"

Her eyes lit up. "Daddy! I open?"

I nodded. "Go ahead, princess."

She beamed with pride as she opened the door, and there stood Willow. Just as beautiful as she always looked, and with a massive smile to boot. Her eyes didn't bother clocking me, though. The second the door swung open, her eyes dropped to my daughter.

Before she crouched down to be eye level with Marie Lee.

"Hi there. I'm Willow. What's your name?"

Marie Lee looked up at me, and I nodded. "It's okay, princess. Go ahead."

She looked down at her feet. "Hi. I'm, uh, Mawie Lee."

Willow smiled. "It's very nice to meet you. I like your socks."

My daughter's eyes whipped up. "You do?"

She nodded. "Yep. I really do. Rainbow is my favorite color."

My daughter pouted. "Daddy say it lots o'cowors. Not one."

Willow lowered her voice to a whisper. "Well, he's wrong, but we won't tell him that. Okay?"

My daughter giggled. "Okay."

My heart beamed with hope. "Come on in. I'm just about to strike up the grill."

Willow stood, but she still didn't look at me. Instead, she held out her hand for my daughter, and I watched Marie Lee slip her tiny hand against Willow's palm. The two of them walked into the house as if they both belonged there, and it was then I made the decision that I'd hire Willow.

But, why not make her sweat it out a bit?

"Can't catch me!" Willow exclaimed.

I closed the front door and watched the girls dart out into the backyard. My daughter chased after Willow as the two of them ran through the kitchen and tore out towards the grass. I chuckled to myself as I gathered everything I needed to throw down a meal on the grill, and I let them have at it. They both stuck their feet in the gated pool and chased each other around the house. Willow picked up my daughter and swung her around before they sat down with colored stacking blocks. I slapped the burgers onto the grill, all the while listening to Willow work with my daughter on the lisp she was developing.

And I wondered how much luckier I'd get in my life after

stumbling across something that seemed so perfect.

So meant to be.

"Lunch is ready!" I exclaimed.

Willow cupped her hands over her mouth. "Food time, Marie Lee!"

My daughter's voice rose above the wind. "Lemonlade, pease!?"

Willow giggled with delight. "I can get you some lemonade, sure!"

A few minutes later, we were all sitting around the glass patio table, diving into our food. None of us talked for a few minutes, but the humming sounds Willow kept making pulled my eyes toward her. She groaned and gave me a thumbs up with every bite of the burger. She placed forkfuls of grilled vegetables into her mouth before promptly making herself another burger. Now, I didn't know much about other men who cooked, but I loved it when someone appreciated my cooking. And Patricia? Well, all she did was nitpick what I cooked.

It was nice to be in the presence of someone who enjoyed it.

"My God, this is so good," Willow said with a sigh.

I grinned. "Glad you like it."

"Swim, Daddy?"

I looked over at my daughter. "You need your swimsuit and floaties. Can you get them out of your room?"

Her eyes lit up. "Yeah! Bye!"

Willow and I laughed together as she disappeared into the house. Then, Willow pointed her finger towards the door.

"Should I go help her?"

I shook my head. "She'll get sidetracked with toys before she even gets to the stairs. It buys us time to work out logistics and stuff."

She paused. "Logistics?"

I crossed my leg over my knee. "Figured you'd wanna talk money. You know, talk about how much the job pays and such."

She nodded. "We can do that now, sure."

I picked up my lemonade. "One of the things I need for Marie Lee right now is consistency and a routine."

"I agree. Those are things any child needs at this age."

"I'm glad we're on the same page. My problem is, I'm worried that she won't get that kind of consistency if the nanny I hire is driving back and forth. You know, rather than living here on the grounds."

She blinked. "You want, I mean, you need a 24-hour nanny?"

"Yes, now that we are talking this through, I believe having someone here, you know, close by would be best for her."

Willow cleared her throat. "Is that building by the pool a guesthouse?"

"It is. And it's one the nanny I hire can occupy while she's, well, nannying Marie Lee."

She nodded slowly. "It's just... It's just something that I

hadn't really considered since it wasn't part of the job description." She waved her hand in the air. "But it's all right. It's best for your daughter. Do you plan on paying weekly? Every two weeks? Once a month?"

"I figured weekly would be fine. Every Monday, I pay for your services, and you enact them. Maybe start around $700 a week, see where we go from there?"

She leaned back in her seat. "Have you given any thought to the P.S. of that email I sent you?"

I tried not to jump out of my skin with excitement. "I have, yes."

"Do you want to discuss that now? Or, is it going to be a hard pass?"

I sipped my lemonade. "I think we could work something out. So long as it doesn't cut into the consistency and routine I want to keep for my daughter."

"Why doesn't your daughter just come to the rodeos? Don't you want to share something that you love with her?"

I paused. "I do, yeah."

"Then, let's take Marie Lee to the rodeos. There's plenty of food there, and I already know she's a fiend like I am for lemonade. I could watch her when I'm not preparing for my event. And, of course, woman's events are before the guys, so she'd be with one of us at all times."

I smiled. "You've been thinking about this."

"Yes, more than a little bit."

I chuckled. "Nothing wrong with that."

"So, other than her routine, what would you say is the

most important thing to you right now regarding your daughter?"

I didn't hesitate. "I want her to know she's safe."

She paused. "Safe?"

I nodded. "Yes. Safe. It's a long story, and one I don't want to get into. But, I got the sneaking suspicion that Marie Lee never quite felt safe sometimes whenever she was in the care of my wi--."

Is she still my wife, though?

I cleared my throat. "My ex-wife. I just got this feeling that maybe my daughter didn't feel too secure when it was just her around. I want her to feel safe, even when I'm not around. That is paramount in this situation."

Willow grinned. "I don't think I'll have a problem with that."

"Oh? Care to elaborate?"

She crossed her legs at her ankles. "I mean, I'm certified in things all nannies should be. CPR. The Heimlich maneuver. Things like that. But, I'm also trained in self-defense techniques, in general. It's not easy being a single woman that lives by herself. So, I come with those types of capabilities as well."

"Is there anything you don't do?"

She reached for her burger. "I don't cook like this. I'm much more prone to baking."

I took pride in watching her enjoy the last bite of her second burger.

"My God, you can throw down," she murmured.

I smiled. "Much appreciated."

She licked her fingers, and I found the movements mesmerizing.

"So, when are you looking for me to move in?" she asked.

I blinked. "Move in?"

She giggled. "Bryce, I don't mean to be forward, but we've talked about what your daughter needs. We've talked about pay. About moving in, and racing your horses, and what we'll do with Marie Lee on the weekends while we're rodeoing. I'm pretty sure you're about to hand me this job."

I snickered. "Are you always so confident?"

"More often than not, yes."

I nodded. "Well, if you want it, the job is yours."

She leaned forward, sticking out her hand. "If you shake, I move in this weekend."

I looked down at her hand. "Under one condition."

"Name it."

I found her stare. "I won't make you sign an NDA, but I need your word you won't talk about the private goings-on of my home, or my work, or my businesses. I don't know what you might be privy to, so I need someone who's not going to make me the first piece of gossip that falls from their lips every morning."

I watched her eyes soften. "You have my word. I'd never do anything like that, especially to a friend."

The authenticity behind her words tugged at my heartstrings. And with one last movement, I shook her hand.

"Welcome aboard, Willow," I said with a broad smile.

She giggled with pride. "Good to be here, Bryce."

7

Willow
Four Days Later

"I still can't believe he gave you this job," Sadie said.

Luna turned around in the passenger's seat. "And so soon. You must be relieved that you won't skip a beat with paychecks."

I smiled, gazing out the back window. "It's nice, yes."

Sadie looked at me in the rearview mirror. "How do you feel about all of this? Moving in and everything?"

I shrugged. "It's only temporary. I'm sure I won't be there for long."

Luna eyed me carefully. "You aren't worried about throwing away money when it comes to the apartment? I mean, you'll be paying rent on a place where you aren't staying."

I snickered. "I'll be able to afford it. He's paying me seven hundred bucks a week to work, plus twenty percent on the side racing every other weekend. One week alone is enough to cover rent, and the rest I pocket. I'm pretty sure that's an awesome deal. I held up my finger. And besides, I can always sublease it if I have too. It's in my lease contract."

Sadie leaned over the steering wheel. "Holy shit. Is this the man's house?"

Luna's jaw dropped open. "Is it a log cabin or something?"

I smiled. "It's a ranch-style home done up like a log cabin. Isn't it gorgeous?"

Bryce's estate really was a sight to behold. His property seemed to stretch on forever, and his neighbors weren't even in sight. The sprawling log cabin, ranch-style home was easily over four thousand square feet, and a pool-slash-hot-tub combination separated the backyard of the main house from the front yard of the guesthouse.

I pointed in front. "Down the gravel driveway. Take the first right-hand off-shoot, and it'll pull us up right to the guesthouse."

Luna rolled down her window. "You mean, that miniature version of this massive house back there?"

I giggled. "That's the one."

Sadie snickered. "Even the guesthouse is huge! How many bedrooms?"

I felt excitement rushing through my veins. "Three

bedrooms, two bathrooms. A full kitchen, living room, and a sliding back door with my own little set of patio furniture. It looks out over the hill that slopes right down to the horse's pasture. It's an incredible view."

Sadie murmured to herself. "Lucky bitch."

I snorted. "I'll pretend I didn't hear that."

I didn't bring much with me to move in. Just my clothes, my toiletries, and a few things that would help me make this place feel more like home: pictures and blankets to throw over the couches. My own bedspread to put on the bed--provided it was a queen-sized bed--and some decorations to hang on the walls. I couldn't wait to get inside and personalize it a bit. Plus, I needed to stock it with groceries.

Maybe some tequila and margarita mix for those nights when I got to sit out back and look out at the horses running around in the pasture below.

Sadie came to a stop by the guesthouse. "Oh. My. God. Look at that pool!"

Luna hopped out of the SUV. "Is that a hot tub?"

I threw my door open. "It sure is."

Sadie opened the trunk with her keys. "I can't wait to have our first girls' night here."

I furrowed my brow. "Well, this is my job. So, I'm not sure how many of those we'll actually have here."

Luna turned to face me. "I mean, surely you've got time off, right?"

Sadie motioned for us to head to the trunk. "I'm sure you've got time off and stuff. It's not like you're a slave to this job. Besides, with three bedrooms, he has to expect you'll have *some* company over. Right?"

I gave her a hard glare. "No. Boys."

Sadie rolled her eyes. "You're not fun."

Luna grabbed one of my clothing bags. "Still, though, on your first night off, we need to come over and christen this place."

I nodded slowly. "Yeah, on my first night off."

As I helped them haul my things into the guesthouse, I felt myself growing wary. Bryce and I hadn't actually discussed things like days off, or even vacation time. Was I privy to something like that with the schedule he wanted me to run with Marie Lee? My knee-jerk reaction for the moment was 'no.'

Would he get upset if I asked about it?

Bryce's voice pulled me from my trance. "You guys need any help!?"

Marie Lee practically shrieked. "Yoo here!"

I heard her giggling as she ran as quickly as she could across the backyard. Bryce was on her heels, ushering her around the pool, so she didn't get sidetracked. I dropped the box I was hauling and held out my arms, watching as the beautiful two-year-old with bouncing curly hair and baby blue eyes ran straight into my arms. Her giggles warmed my soul. Her soft hug around my neck with her little baby arms made my soul take flight with happiness. I covered her cheeks in kisses, listening as she laughed so hard she started wheezing.

And as Bryce picked up the box beside me, I saw Sadie and Luna practically drooling over him.

"Down, girls," I warned.

And my words earned a hearty chuckle from Bryce himself.

"Snack?" Marie Lee asked.

I bopped her nose softly with my finger. "Hungry, huh?"

"Carrots?"

My eyebrows rose. "Do you like carrots?"

She nodded heartily. "And tornadoes."

I blinked. "Tomatoes?"

She paused. "The red fings?"

"Yes, tomatoes. Can you say that?"

She furrowed her brow. "Tomatoes."

"Toe-may-toes."

She focused on me. "Toe-may-toes."

I smiled. "Right! Tomatoes."

She threw her hands in the air. "Tormaynoes!"

I threw my head back with laughter before I carried her into the guesthouse. I carried her into the kitchen and surveyed the barren wasteland that was this empty place. Which meant I needed to have groceries delivered. While Bryce unloaded the rest of my things while the girls ogled him like lovesick puppies, I pulled out my phone and opened up the Instacart app.

And twenty minutes later, I had a kitchen full of groceries headed in my direction.

"All right. Want to go see if there are any tomatoes in the kitchen?" I asked.

Marie Lee paused. "This not kitchen?"

I giggled. "It is a kitchen. But, it doesn't have any food in it yet."

Bryce stuck his head around the corner. "Need me to order some?"

I craned my eyes over my shoulder. "I already got them coming. Could you stay and receive them, though? Marie Lee wants some tomatoes, and I don't know when the groceries are actually going to arrive."

He nodded. "I can do that. Want me to unpack any of your stuff?"

I paused. "Leave the bags. Those are my clothes. But, the boxes have things you can unpack. Just pictures and blankets and stuff I brought with me. I think one has a queen-sized bed sheet set in it."

He chuckled. "That might not work on the king-sized beds that are in here."

I could hear the girls practically squealing as they stood in the corner, watching the two of us interact.

"Well, then just toss it in a closet somewhere, I guess," I said with a wave of my hand.

It shocked me that Bryce seemed to be in such good spirits. His smiles were genuine, and he was eager to help out any way he could. And all the while, I wondered what kind of hurt he was covering up. As Marie Lee laid her head on my shoulder, I watched Bryce dig into the first box he found. I found myself focusing on his arms. His muscles, undulating beneath his skin. His pert ass jutted out every time he bent over for the entire world to behold. My head fell off to the side as I mindlessly bounced Marie Lee in my arms. But, it was Sadie clearing her throat that ripped me from my trance.

"I'm glad you're settled in, but now Luna and I have to get out of here. We have some shopping to do ourselves," she said.

I blinked. "Yes, yes. I'm so sorry. Let me hug you girls first. Thank you so much for helping me out."

I hugged their necks tightly before Luna pressed her lips to my ear.

"Don't do anything Sadie wouldn't do."

I grinned. "Doesn't leave much, Luna."

Sadie piped up from the door. "I heard that!"

I gave Luna one more hug before I ushered them back to the car. While Bryce continued to unpack boxes, I waved the girls off. Then, I finally took Marie Lee inside and got her a small bowl of cherry tomatoes. It took me a little bit to figure out that she wanted to drown them in ranch dressing. But, was there really any other way to eat cherry tomatoes?

"Want one?" she asked.

And when Marie Lee held out a dripping tomato for me to eat, pain filled my gut.

"I'd love one. Thank you," I said.

How in the world would anyone leave such a beautiful girl behind? I'd only spent a short amount of time with her, but I was already in love with her. How Bryce's ex-wife--or, soon to be ex wife?--could leave behind her own daughter was beyond me. Just to ditch the entire family you've created for another man? It made me ache for them both.

For Marie Lee, and for Bryce.

"I promise never to leave you," I whispered.

And when she smiled at me with those ranch-covered cheeks, she stole my heart all over again.

Heavy footfalls came up behind me. "Looks like a good snack. Mind if I join?"

I turned around at the sound of Bryce's voice. "Sure. Want some tomatoes with your ranch, like your daughter over here?"

Marie Lee smiled brightly. "Hi, Daddy."

He chuckled. "Hi, princess."

I watched him walk over to his daughter and ruffle her hair, to which she grimaced up at him. It would've made me laugh, too, if Bryce didn't look so sizzling hot in the jeans he wore. His sleeves were rolled up, showcasing the veins protruding from his sunkissed forearms. And when he flashed me that pearly white smile of his, I noticed something.

He and his daughter had the same baby blue eyes.

"You hungry, Willow?" he asked.

The sound of my name on his voice made the hairs on the nape of my neck stand on end.

This isn't good. Don't make the mistake you did with Morris.

I swallowed hard. "I'm good, but thanks. I can get you something, though?"

He shook his head. "You're the nanny. Not the butler. I can get my own snack. Thanks for offering, though."

Marie Lee held up another tomato. "Here, Daddy."

He took it. "Thanks, princess."

And when he plopped it into his mouth, I couldn't help but watch his tongue swipe over the ranch sitting against his lower lip.

Making me hot between my legs as I sat there, trying not to fall for yet another boss.

8

Bryce

I laid in my bed, staring up at the ceiling. I couldn't think straight. Hell, I could hardly see straight. And despite my long days, taxed with physical and mental exhaustion, I still couldn't get a good night's sleep. Between training horses, helping my brothers run the family petroleum company, and raising my daughter, one would have figured sleep would come easy for me. That I'd hit the bed, fall asleep, and not move until the sun came up. However, as nighttime hung heavily outside, I found myself reaching for my phone to check the time.

And groaned when I saw it was damn near midnight.

"Damn it," I murmured.

I couldn't stop thinking about my wife. About that note.

About the fact that she had abandoned our daughter. Someone was sleeping with her, and that man had defiled my family with his actions. Fury boiled my blood as I sat up straight. I threw the covers off my legs and slipped my feet into my slippers. I had practically memorized that note she left behind—the only remnant of the fact that I'd ever had a wife in the first place. I mean, fucking hell, the woman cleaned out her damn closet when she left. She took her clothes and her shoes and her trinkets and erased all pieces of her in this house. I wasn't sure I'd ever forgive her for it. But, there was one person I was much angrier at.

And that was the man who thought he could break up my family.

I stormed over to my desk in the corner and opened my laptop. I pushed away the fact that Patricia hadn't called all week. I pushed aside the fact that Marie Lee didn't once ask where her mother had gone. I even pushed away the fact that it didn't take much for Patricia to erase her existence from this house. I mean, she hadn't once helped me decorate or hang a picture. She wasn't in any of the 'family photos' I wanted to put up on the walls. Without her clothes and her massive collection of shoes, no one would've even known there was a woman in this house in the first place.

The thought made me sick.

Had I done wrong by Patricia? I thought I had been doing the right thing by marrying her when we figured out we were pregnant. That's what any self-respecting man of my upbringing would have done. She was the mother of my child, for crying out loud! Of course, I'd stick by her through thick and thin. She ripped her entire body open and gave up whatever future she saw for herself to have my child. I'd bend over backward for her any day of the week.

And this is the thanks I got from her?

"I want to know who this man is," I grumbled to myself.

At damn near midnight, I started my search. I wanted to know who the fuck she was doing that was more important than her own child. I wanted to know who the hell had her attention so fixated that she completely forgot to call and check up on her own flesh and blood. So, I typed away on my computer, trying to find any shred of evidence that might point me in the right direction.

"Come on, Facebook," I murmured.

I scrolled endlessly through her pictures of the sunset outside in our backyard and mindless pictures of her and Marie Lee. And the one thing I found in all of those pictures was the fact that her smile was fake. The corners of her smile never quite reached her eyes, and I found it more unnerving than anything. It seemed too blatant in all of the pictures, so why didn't I see it in real-time?

Had Patricia been miserable all this time?

Her note ran through my head as I logged into Instagram. I wasn't a social media user, but I did have business accounts. And those business accounts had my wife added to them. I scrolled through her endless selfies and pictures of cocktails at two in the afternoon she'd had Maria make her, and part of me wanted to cry out in anger. My wife, drinking at two in the afternoon with our daughter sitting on the floor in the background, seemingly in tears. My hands trembled in fury and anguish at how lost my daughter felt in the presence of her own mother.

But still, I apparently hadn't been as present of a husband--or as present of a father--as I thought I had been. Because if I had been, I would've seen all of this. I would've seen the pictures on Instagram and the fake smile she plastered all over Facebook. I would've seen it with my own eyes had I not been working so damn much and just said 'no' to a rodeo or two in order to spend the weekend with my family.

You're an idiot, Bryce.

After her social media profiles yielded nothing regarding the man she had left me for, I started a new Google search. The search? 'Private investigator near me.' And that's all it took. The very first entry was for a man by the name of 'Detective Ryan Peterson', and judging by his testimonials, he was very good at what he did. I looked around his website before finding the contact form down at the very bottom, and I sent him a quick inquiry.

...At almost one in the morning.

"Jesus," I sighed.

I gave him a brief rundown of the situation: the fact that my wife had left me for another man. Abandoned her daughter, and was nowhere to be found. I let him know a bit about our situation, that we got married after a one-night stand left her pregnant, and I had tried to do right by her. But, when it came time to state the outcome I wanted for this investigation, I drew a blank.

What did I want to come from all this?

Did I want Patricia back? My heart didn't, no. I mean, I respected the woman. She was the mother of my child. But did I love her? No. If I was being honest with myself, I didn't. I never had. I had love for her, but I wasn't in love with her if that made any sense. And as I stared at the blinking cursor, it occurred to me. For once in my life, I knew what I wanted.

I wanted to figure out if Patricia wanted anything to do with our daughter.

After hitting 'send' and watching the inquiry whoosh off into the nethersphere of the internet, I slowly turned around in my chair. I stared at my massive bed that seemed emptier than usual, and a sudden wave of exhaustion hit me. I leaned back in my leather chair and ran my hands down my face. The only thing I could do right now was exactly what I'd just done, and for some reason, that made me angry again. After everything I'd done for that woman and everything I had sacrificed, the only thing I could do was send a message pouring my heart and soul out to some random asshole on the internet before I had her stalked to figure out what the fuck she was doing that was more important than her own damn daughter.

I stood to my feet as my hands trembled with rage.

Without anything better to do, I changed into my bathing suit. I ripped a towel out of my linen closet and made my way downstairs, not stopping until I got outside. I tossed my towel down onto a lounge chair and raked my hand through my hair. The full moon hovered heavily in the sky, casting a soft glow of radiant blue around my backyard. I watched the stars twinkle on top of the water in my pool as I reached my foot over toward a red button. And when I pressed it, the hot tub beside me roared to life.

Then, I dove straight into the pool and started swimming some laps.

I took all my pent-up energy and threw it into swimming. I paddled and kicked as hard as I could, feeling my heart rate skyrocket. I heaved for air every time I turned my head, then I dove underwater and pushed off the wall again. Every time the hot tub stopped roiling with bubbles, I jumped up enough to slap that damn button with my hand. And after swimming until I couldn't catch my breath, I pushed myself up onto the edge of the hot tub that connected to the pool and tumbled in headfirst.

When I came up, though, a flickering light caught the corner of my eye. I continued to pant for air as I sat on the bench against the wall of the hot tub, my eyes trailing over to the guesthouse. I watched another light turn off, and I furrowed my brow tightly. And as I watched a shadow pass quickly by a window before turning off the last light, I paused.

What in the world was Willow doing up at this hour?

Is she all right?

As the bubbles burst against my skin, my mind started to run away from me. Maybe she'd been watching me swim. Maybe I'd woken her up with my furious swimming, and she had come to take a peek at me. A grin spread across my face at the idea. Maybe she wanted to get in with me and swim but was too timid to come out of her own volition. Should I go knock on her door and invite her out?

Could I even stand to see those thick curves of hers in a swimsuit?

You're still married, Bryce. Cool those jets.

I drew in a sobering breath and decided to head back inside because if I stayed out here any longer, I'd end up doing something absolutely stupid. It didn't matter that Patricia had left. It didn't matter that she had another man on the side, and for God only knew how long, too. All that mattered were my morals. And until I was at least separated officially from her, there wasn't a woman that could get me to touch her.

I still felt my mind wandering, though.

"Time to get out," I murmured to myself.

As the bubbles slowed to a stop, I pushed myself out of the tub. I walked quickly over to my towel half-hanging on the ground and scooped it up as I made my way toward the porch. I forced myself not to look over my shoulder. I forced myself to keep my eyes straight. Because the last thing I needed was to question myself enough to double-back and knock on her door.

Oh, how I wanted to, though.

I made my way upstairs and dried myself off, slipping out of my bathing suit. I hung it up in my bathroom before tossing my towel into the dirty clothes hamper, then jumped back into bed. I pulled the covers over my naked body and closed my eyes, trying to will myself to go back to sleep. And even though the exhaustion from swimming had me dead tired, Willow's saucy curves kept me awake.

The idea of her warmth against me kept my muscles locked.

The delectable outline of her thickness made my mouth water. My hands tremble. My cock stiffened.

Horses. Think of horses, and Will training them. Mud. Mud is dirty. Mud isn't hot at all. Unless Willow's rolling around in it.

My eyes snapped open, and I cursed myself for being so weak. And as I laid there, my body begging my brain to shut off, I watched the sheet over my body slowly tent itself.

Seemingly unaware of the fact that I was still a married man.

Fuck.

9

Willow

B*womp! Bwomp! Bwomp! Bwomp! Bwomp!*

I groaned as my eyes slowly slid open. My hand reached over and slapped the screen of my phone, shutting the damn thing off. I groaned as I laid there, trying to get my tired body to move. But, because of my unintentional late night last night, it was hard to move, especially after falling asleep with Bryce on my mind.

Nevertheless, I forced myself to sit up. It didn't matter that I'd only gotten four hours of sleep. The only thing that mattered was the fact that I needed to be in the house and upstairs in less than an hour. Thank the Lord, I showered before I went to bed last night. My snooze alarm went off again, filling the room with that blaring sound that always rattled me awake with a start. I reached for my phone again, turning the alarm off completely. Then I started to get into my clothes for the day before making it through the back patio doors around 6:45.

As I carried the baby monitor with me, I made my way into the kitchen. Marie Lee hadn't gotten up yet, so I took the liberty of starting a pot of coffee. I knew that after Bryce's late-night swim, he'd need a cup, and I sure as hell needed one, too. So, after getting it started and filling the kitchen with the decadent smell of imported coffee from Ecuador, Marie Lee started whining over the baby monitor.

So, I rushed up the stairs and barreled into her room.

"Good morning, pretty girl," I said with a smile.

Marie Lee looked up at me with tired eyes. "Eggs?"

I scooped her out of her bed. "Sure, we can have some eggs. Wanna go wake Daddy up first?"

She smiled sleepily. "Da-da in bed."

I giggled. "Yes, he is. Daddy is in bed."

As I bounced the beautiful little girl in my arms, I went and knocked on Bryce's door. Right at seven, just like he wanted, and I knocked away until I heard him shuffling around. A grumble sounded behind the door, and his gravelly voice sent a shiver down my spine. Nevertheless, I kept my voice as even as I could.

"Wake up call, Bryce. I've got coffee on downstairs."

He groaned. "Thanks."

I grinned to myself as I made my way back downstairs. With Marie Lee resting her head against my shoulder, I pressed my cheek softly against her tangled curls. I heard the front door open just as I crossed through the foyer, signaling to me that Maria--the wonderful cook and impeccable cleaner of the household--had arrived.

"And what will we be having for breakfast?" Maria asked in that thick Spanish accent I loved so dearly.

I smiled. "Eggs for the little one."

She smiled. "And for the big one?"

I glared at her playfully. "Hey, I'm working on it."

"You don't have to do a thing, Miss Willow. You're perfect the way you are."

"You know you can call me 'Willow.' No 'Miss,' if you don't want to."

She snickered. "Habit, Miss Willow. But, if it makes you feel better, you can call me 'Miss Maria.'"

"Miss Maria, it is. And for breakfast, I usually just have coffee."

Maria shook her head. "I'll make you some eggs, too. And toast?"

Marie Lee's head shot up from my shoulder. "Butter bread!"

Maria pointed to her. "Butter bread it is, sweet girl."

I kissed the top of Marie Lee's head. "Let's go get ready for the day, and then we'll come eat. Sound good?"

She smiled at me, and my heart melted. "Yeah."

I kissed the tip of her nose. "Great. Let's go. Because your breath stinkies."

She giggled. "Stinky winky! Stinky winky!"

I laughed all the way back up the stairs and slipped into the bathroom across the hall from Marie Lee's room. And as I helped the small girl brush her teeth, I heard Bryce lumbering down the hallway. I forced myself to keep my focus on his daughter, despite the fact that I felt him pause at the bathroom door. What he was doing, I wasn't sure. But, as Marie Lee spit out the toothpaste into the sink, I felt my cheeks flushing.

It felt like Bryce was staring, but I didn't have the guts to turn around and see if my gut was right.

"Beh-fast time!" Marie Lee exclaimed.

I picked her up. "Yes. After we get you dressed, okay?"

She pouted. "Buh, butter bread?"

I booped her nose. "After we get dressed. I'll even let you dress yourself. How does that sound?"

Her eyes lit up. "Dress! Pink!"

I nodded. "Your pink dress, it is."

I carried the excited little girl into her room and let her run around, picking out her outfit. She brought me a beautiful pink sundress with rainbow-colored shoes and a black bow to put in her hair, and I obliged without a second thought. She was so wonderful and so independent and so funny at such a young age, and I wanted to encourage that within her. I wanted to encourage that fiery spirit I'd gotten to know my first full week here at my new job.

But, when we went back downstairs to have breakfast, I found Bryce sitting at the table. Right next to my plate of food. Sipping a cup of coffee while he read something on his phone.

And as I stared at him with his daughter in my arms, I couldn't shake the memory of him last night.

He looked absolutely amazing, swimming around in that pool. His muscles, dripping with water. His hair, trickling down his forehead and leading my eyes to his strong jawline. His body, slick with water while the lines of his muscles glistened in the moonlight. Oh, how I had wanted to join him last night. Oh, how I had wanted to get in that hot tub with him and just soak. But, I hadn't wanted to impose on him, nor did I want to make the same mistake twice.

He was my boss. And after staying up last night crying over Dr. Morris, the last thing I needed was to get involved with yet another one of my bosses. The rejection alone hurt enough. But, I didn't want to compromise Marie Lee with my selfish actions. If it was just me who might have gotten hurt, I would've taken the opportunity. There was an innocent soul at stake here, though. And I wanted to do right by her.

Plus, I had enough on my mind. The memory of Dr. Morris and how he looked at me with disgust broke my confidence down last night enough to make me poke at my curves in the mirror before I fell asleep. Which was big for me, because I had always prided myself in my thickness. In the way, men stared at me while holding the hands of their skinny little girlfriends. Men could pretend all they wanted, but they loved the way I was shaped. The way my hips swayed. The way my thighs blossomed and the way my breasts sat heavily against my chest—no man passed by me without looking at least once. But, for a brief moment last night, I let Dr. Morris' words get inside my head.

Causing me to poke at my curves instead of admiring them.

Thank the Lord sleep did me some good.

"Willow!"

I jumped at the sound of Bryce's voice. "Yes?"

He furrowed his brow. "Your food's getting cold. Want me to heat up your coffee?"

I looked over at my food. "No, no. It's fine. Marie Lee? Ready to eat?"

I peeked over at the beautiful little girl and saw her nodding her head vigorously. And the sight of her beautiful bouncing curls made me giggle.

"All right," I said as I walked her over to her seat, "let's get you some food, then."

But, it wasn't long before I sat down beside Bryce that he piped up next to me.

"I saw your lights on last night while I was swimming. You okay?"

His question warmed my heart, and it almost sounded as if he cared. "Yeah, just up late."

He snickered. "Trouble sleeping?"

I reached for my coffee. "It happens sometimes. Just got a lot on my mind."

He shook his head. "Sounds like me last night."

I looked over at him. "Are you all right?"

And when his eyes met mine, I saw pain rushing behind his stare.

It gave me pause as I gazed into his gorgeous baby blue eyes. Marie Lee had inherited those eyes, and I couldn't turn away from them. The soft smile on his face might've painted a different picture, but I knew that look. I knew that gaze. He was hurt, and rightfully so. And it hurt my soul that such a beautiful man had been wronged in such a horrible way.

"I'll be fine," he said, his gaze falling quickly back to his phone.

I sipped my coffee. "Fair enough."

We all ate in relative silence as Maria started cleaning up the kitchen first. I knew her routine already like the back of my hand, which allowed me to tailor Marie Lee's schedule to hers. After breakfast came reading time in the living room while Maria cleaned the back patio. And after Maria came inside, Marie Lee and I headed up to her room where we did our reading and learning time. It didn't take long for me to get this beautiful little two-year-old on a schedule that worked for her. But, today? Things felt a little different.

Namely, I felt Bryce watching me more than usual.

Granted, it was a Saturday, and it was one of the very few Saturdays where there wasn't a rodeo going on in town. I still figured the man would have work to accomplish, but apparently not. Because every room Marie Lee and I occupied while Maria worked, Bryce seemed to be there. If we were outside, he was sitting on the back porch. If we were in Marie Lee's room, he was walking up and down the hallway between his study and his bedroom. If Marie Lee and I were watching a movie in the living room, he was in the kitchen, rummaging around for something.

And all the while, I felt his eyes on me.

I wanted to ask him several times if he wanted to join us. But, I resisted the urge. Partially because I didn't want to throw Marie Lee off her routine, but mostly because I wouldn't have been asking Bryce to join us for her benefit. I'd be doing it for me, and that wasn't fair. I liked the fact that Bryce wanted to watch me. I liked the fact that Bryce kept finding himself in our presence with every step of the day. I liked the fact that he kept gravitating to me, whether or not he realized it.

What I didn't like was how much it tempted me. What I didn't like was how much I wanted to cave to it. And what I hated was how eager I was to lay Marie Lee back down tonight.

Because I knew if I got Bryce alone again, I'd have more balls than I did last night.

Which wouldn't bode well for anyone involved.

10

Bryce

I felt my brother's eyes on the back of my head as I continued typing away at my computer. It had been a couple of weeks since I'd hired Willow to help me, and my brother had been giving me the side-eye ever since. Why? I wasn't sure. But, I wouldn't give into his game. Either he brought up the topic on his own, or it didn't get discussed.

And in good ol' Will Remington fashion, he talked around it.

"So, how have things been since Patricia packed up?"

I bit back my disgust. "Fine."

He pulled up a chair next to me. "Just fine?"

I continued typing away. "Yep."

"Right. And... and I take it you're trying to figure out who this man is that she left you for?"

"Either spit it out or leave it, Will."

He sighed. "I'm just trying to get you to talk to me, Bryce. That so bad?"

I swiveled away from my desk and looked him straight in the face. "No, you're not. You're trying to get confirmation or denial based on the things you've heard in town. You're probably being bombarded with questions you don't have answers to, so now you're looking for answers."

"I can be concerned and curious at the same time."

I turned back toward my computer. "You're a worse gossip than most women in this town, you know that?"

"Oh, come on, give me a bit of credit. It's been over two weeks since your wife left you, and you haven't so much as spoken about it. That weirds me out."

"I don't talk about a lot of things, and you've never been weirded out before."

"Because I don't ever speak up. But, we aren't talking about Marie Lee swallowing things she shouldn't or some fight you had with Patricia. We're talking about your wife leaving and you suddenly moving in some hot-ass nanny to take care of your daughter? Why don't you just take time off work? Actually spend it with your daughter instead of trying t--."

I growled. "Are you trying to tell me how to parent my child?"

Will held up his hands. "I'm just trying to get you to see

that your whole 'bury yourself in work when shit gets rough' thing doesn't always end up healthy for others involved."

I sighed. "You're right."

He paused. "I'm what? I mean, yeah. Of course, I'm right."

I chuckled bitterly. "I can't sleep, Will."

"I can only imagine."

I slowly swiveled to face him again. "I can't sleep, I'm hardly eating, and Willow? The Nannie I've hired? She's been the only bright spot in all this. She's good with Marie Lee, she keeps us on a schedule. I mean, her presence is the only presence that makes me feel like I might actually make it out of this."

He nodded slowly. "Have you heard from Pat at all?"

I shook my head. "Not one peep. Not even to check on her own daughter."

"I always knew that woman was a slimy, conniving little snake."

"But more than that, it kills me that I don't know who she's left me for. It kills me that she was fucking around behind my back while I gave up so much of myself to make this family work. It makes me wonder if she even cared about making this work in the first place."

"You two got pregnant, and then you got married. It's not like anyone had high hopes for you two."

I scoffed. "Thanks."

"I'm just being serious. Maybe she's actually found someone she loves. Can you really blame her for that?"

"Could she not have loved me?"

"You were a one-night stand, Bryce. Can you honestly look me in my eyes and tell me that you love that woman?"

I closed my eyes. "No."

"For all you know, she's fallen in love."

"And left her daughter behind to pursue it."

He sat back in his chair. "I didn't say she was in the right. I just said there might be other emotions at play that you *both* deserve."

I raked my hands down my face. "So, hiring a P.I. to figure out who the hell she's with wasn't such a good idea?"

And when silence filled the room, I opened my eyes.

"Will?" I asked.

He blinked. "Did you just say you hired someone to follow her around until you find out who's sleeping with her?"

"Well, when you put it like that…"

"What the fuck is wrong with you, dude? Just move on! She's given you an out, and I know damn good and well how miserable you were in that marriage."

"It wasn't all bad, Will."

"Yeah, just every other weekend and most Wednesdays. Right?"

I pinched the bridge of my nose. "I gave this woman my future, man. I gave the entire rest of my life to her to do the right thing, and she throws it in my face like this?"

"Why do you even care enough to track her like this? You can't even say you love her. Why the fuck do you care?"

"I care for Marie Lee!" I bellowed.

And when Will nodded, I knew he finally understood.

"Will, one day, my daughter's gonna want answers. She's going to want to know what the hell's happened to her mother. And I'm not going to know what to tell her. I want to make sure I can give that to her. Because as the days roll on when her mother doesn't come back, I start to wonder if she'll *ever* come back. Not for me, but for her."

He grinned. "Sure, this isn't about that hot nanny you've hired?"

My face fell. "You're a fuckwad, you know that?"

"Oh, come on! Let me live a little. The entire town's talking about it!"

I turned back to my computer. "I'm done with this conversation."

"Look, all I'm saying is that if you don't love her, then maybe you're trying to find proof that Pat has really moved on so you can, too. You know, with the hot curvy chick living in your house."

"Guesthouse," I murmured.

He barked with laughter. "Anyway, I can tell you're drained so I'll leave it be."

"Should've done that ten minutes ago."

"You got a reason as to why we're preparing one of our other mares for the upcoming rodeo?"

And when I fell silent, Will snickered.

"She's racing our horses now, isn't she?" he asked.

My fingers started clicking across the keyboard. "It's part of her hiring package."

He chuckled. "Told you so."

His dumbass voice grated on my nerves so much that I took a swing at him. And when he rolled his chair back, all he did was laugh his ass off. I glared at him as I watched him prance out of my office then I forced myself to get back to work. I had to get this paperwork submitted for the rodeo before I missed the deadline and went defunct on my contract with Willow.

But, around two in the afternoon--just as I went to pack up and go train--a knock came at my office door.

"Come in," I called out.

The door swung open without a sound, so I turned to see who it was. As my computer powered down and I slung my bag over my shoulder, I watched some needle-nosed kid with a crooked tie pull something out of a bag at his side. With the worn shoulder strap rubbing against his faded black suit jacket, his jeans left much to be desired. But, when he handed me a manilla envelope stacked with papers, I swallowed hard.

"I'm sorry, Mr. Remington," the boy said.

I watched aimlessly as he scurried out of my office. I looked down at the envelope that had my name on it. I recognized that handwriting, too. It was Pat's handwriting.

And when I opened it up, I slid out an official copy of divorce papers...Papers she had already signed.

I roared with anger as I threw the stack of papers at the wall. They scattered everywhere, raining down upon the floor as I drew in another lungful of air. I bellowed my anger for the four walls of my office to absorb, and when I felt my voice finally giving out, I flopped back down into my seat.

I can't train today.

I wasn't sure how long I sat there, but once a cooler head prevailed, I scooped up the papers. I didn't know what order they were in, and I didn't care. All I did was shove them into my desk and locked up for the day. I tore home in a frenzied state, blowing through yellow lights and rolling stop signs as if it were my actual day job. And when I got home, all I wanted was to crawl into bed and act as if the world outside didn't exist.

That didn't happen, though.

Instead, when I opened the front door of my home, I heard music blaring from the living room. The sounds of my daughter's voice singing at the top of her lungs filled my ears, and I silently dropped my bag to the floor. I eased the front door closed and silenced my footsteps, walking through the foyer just to peek around the corner. And when I saw Willow swinging my daughter around to the beat of the music coming from our Disney-plus channel, I smiled.

I genuinely smiled.

Instantly, my anger melted into nothingness. I'd never seen such a big smile on my daughter's face before. Usually, when I walked into the house, I walked into either Marie Lee sleeping or crying about something. But, never this. That thought made the smile melt from my face, though. Clearly, Willow's influence in her life was much more positive than her own mothers'.

So, what would happen once Patricia got custody of Marie Lee?

I can't let that happen.

My daughter had to stay with me, no matter the cost.

"Daddy! Come!"

Marie Lee's voice pulled me from my trance, and I watched Willow whip around. A crooked smile crossed my face as Willow held out her hand for me, beckoning me to join their little dance party. Even in just two weeks, my daughter talked more around Willow than she had in the first two years of her life. Her language was blossoming, she was becoming more outgoing, and as I walked into the living room to scoop my daughter into her arms, I felt her press a kiss against my cheek.

A show of affection my daughter rarely bestowed upon anyone.

"Hi, Daddy," she said, laying her head on my shoulder.

I kissed her soft curls. "Hey there, princess."

Willow smiled. "You're home early."

I nodded. "Felt like coming home a bit early."

Marie Lee sat up. "Snack?"

I grinned. "I suppose--."

Willow cut me off. "Uh, uh, uh. You know when snack time is, pretty girl. And you know now's not it."

Willow plucked a pouting Marie Lee from my arms, and I was very impressed with how easily my daughter obeyed despite her not being happy with the outcome.

"Well, what if we work up an appetite?" I asked.

Marie Lee smiled. "Yeah! Teh-tites!"

Willow crooked an eyebrow. "How so?"

I smiled. "What if we dance around and burn off all those calories for an early snack? That might work, right, Miss Willow?"

Marie Lee looked up at her. "Pwease, Mish Willow?"

She cast me a knowing look. "I suppose. But, we have to dance really, really hard. Can you do that for me?"

And as my daughter nodded her head with glee, I joined the two of them in a dance. Twirling around, jumping up and down, and somehow ending up with Willow in my arms.

My strength, wrapped around her waist.

Her eyes, gazing into mine.

And for a brief moment, nothing in the world mattered anymore. Not the divorce papers, not Pat, and certainly not my businesses.

11

Willow

Bryce stabbed at his steak. "So, princess. What were you and Willow up to today?"

Marie Lee smiled through her french fries. "Swim."

"Oh, you two went swimming. Did you have fun?"

She nodded her head with glee as I reached for my glass of wine.

"What else did you guys do?" Bryce asked.

Marie Lee swallowed hard. "Nap."

"Ah, good ol' nap time. I could've used one of those today. What was your favorite part of today?"

She threw her ketchup-stained hands into the air. "Dance!"

I giggled. "Mine, too, pretty girl."

I caught Bryce's eyes across the table from me, and I tried my best not to blush. But, the truth of the matter was our dance party had ended well over three hours ago, and I still felt the warmth of his embrace around my waist. The dance had been so innocent, the touch, so soft. And I couldn't get it out of my mind. It was as if he had cursed me, entrancing me, just with the stroke of his fingertips against the dip of my waist.

I'm in biiiiig trouble.

I watched as Marie Lee babbled on to her father about the day we had, and all the while I struggled not to stare. Watching them interact with one another warmed me to my core, and I simply couldn't imagine the kind of crazy a woman would have to be in order to leave all of this behind. What a wonderful and giving situation they had going on here. Prosperous financially. A handsome husband. A beautiful, kind, loving daughter. Maria, to help out with the cooking and the cleaning. It was a woman's dream life! How in the world would someone leave it?

Leave them?

It made me sick to my stomach to think about.

"Penny for your thoughts," Bryce said.

His voice ripped me from my trance, and I found both him and Marie Lee staring at me.

"Oh, just planning out tomorrow. That's all," I said.

"Swim?" Marie Lee asked.

I winked at her. "If it doesn't storm, okay?"

My eyes met Bryce's again, and when he smiled at me, I felt my stomach flutter. I shot him a kind grin before my eyes dropped to my food, and I did all I could to focus on my eating. I had hardly touched my perfectly-grilled steak, which wasn't like me. Steak and seafood, those were my two favorite foods. So, I should've been scarfing this thing down without a care in the world.

Instead, though, my focus was on how close Bryce's feet were to mine underneath the dinner table.

Thankfully, dinner was over sooner rather than later, and I took the opportunity to put some distance between us. I scooped up a very messy Marie Lee while Bryce cleared the table, giving Maria an early evening. I walked the beautiful little girl upstairs and got her ready for her bath before playing 'pirates and sharks' with her toys. Then, we brushed her hair, brushed her teeth, and I let her pick out her pajamas.

Just like we had done every night for the past two weeks.

"Princess!" she exclaimed.

I pulled out her princess dress. "You want to sleep in this again?"

She nodded her head furiously. "Uh-huh, uh-huh."

"Hmmm, let me think about it."

"Pweeeeease!?" she begged.

I put my tongue against my two front teeth. "Luh, luh, luh. Do that with me."

Marie Lee mocked me. "Luh, luh, luh."

"P-luh-ease."

"P-luh-ease."

"Please."

Her eyes grew big as saucers. "Pwease?"

I giggled. "We'll work on it, okay?"

"Yes?"

I nodded. "Yes. You can wear the dress."

"Yessssss!"

She threw her fists into the air, and I quickly slid the dress over her head. It didn't take long to get her into it, then I tucked her beneath her princess sheets and comforter. Marie Lee still wasn't at a point where she wanted me to read her a bedtime story. But, we had gotten more comfortable with me holding her hand until she fell asleep.

And once her hand went limp in mine, I stood up and turned off the light so her Olaf night light would glow and make her feel safe.

"Night, pretty girl," I whispered.

Then, I closed the door and made my way downstairs.

"Thought you might want another glass," Bryce said.

I jumped at the sound of his voice, and his low chuckle rattled my ribcage. My widened eyes whipped over toward the kitchen, where he stood there with a full glass of wine in his hand. He walked it over to me, and I took it, thankful to drown my nerves in the relaxing alcohol.

But, when he continued to stand there and sip on his own glass, I furrowed my brow.

"Is everything all right?" I asked.

He held his hand out toward the couch. "Mind if we talk for a bit?"

I peeked over my shoulder. "Uh, sure. What about?"

Instead of answering me, though, he simply ushered me over to the couch. With his hand pressed against the small of my back, it grew hard for me to breathe until he finally pulled away. I sank to the cushions and took a long pull from my drink, hoping it might calm my nerves. But, when Bryce sat on the cushion right next to mine instead of on the opposite side of the couch, I forgot all about the wine glass I started clutching a bit too tightly.

"You're worrying me," I said softly.

He grinned. "I don't mean to. I just thought we might want to get to know each other a little more since things are really working out with you here."

I felt oddly... disappointed? "Oh."

"Oh?"

I sipped my wine. "Well, what would you like to know?"

He shrugged. "Anything you'd like me to know."

"Oh."

"There you go with that tone of voice again."

I snickered. "It's nothing bad. Just getting a feel for the situation."

"Are you uncomfortable?"

I paused. "No, actually. I'm not. Just... stepping with caution."

"Have I given you a reason to?"

Other than being drop-dead gorgeous? "Not really?"

He set his wine glass on the coffee table. "Look, Marie Lee has really taken to you. And the last thing I want is to upend a schedule she seems to have created with you. But, everyone has a past. And I just want to make sure there's nothing about you that will--."

I held up my hand. "Say no more. I understand."

"Is there anything I should be worried about?"

Should I tell him? Would he fire me if I told him? Did he already know, and this was his way of approaching things? I knew it was better to tell the truth, but I was worried the truth might cost me my job. I couldn't fault him for wanting to suss things out, though. So, I decided to be upfront and honest.

"Safe space?" I asked.

He nodded. "Safe space."

"No judgment?"

"None at all. Even if this weren't a safe space, which it is."

I set my wine down next to his. "All right, then. There is something you should know."

"I'm all ears."

I drew in a deep breath. "Right up until I quit my job, Dr. Morris and I were sleeping together."

He blinked. "Oh."

I giggled. "Yeah. Oh."

"He--you--uh..."

"I'm really sorry. I promise you, it wasn't something either of us intended. It just--."

He held up his hand. "For how long?"

I sighed. "Around six months? Maybe a bit more?"

"Were you two dating?"

I shook my head. "I thought we were? I mean, in the beginning, he wanted to keep things on the down-low because I was his employee, and I got that. But, I suppose I figured it wouldn't always be that way."

"If you don't mind me asking, why did you quit?"

I scoffed bitterly. "Well, I was also racing his horses. He gave me the opportunity to get back into barrel racing after my last sponsor dropped me because I *wouldn't* sleep with him, so I figured why not? Well, with all the rich dinners and late-night dessert runs we did together, I put on some weight, and--."

"You're kidding."

My eyes found his. "What?"

He narrowed his eyes. "He used your weight as an excuse to break up with you?"

"No, no, no, no. At least, well--. I mean, he wanted me to stop racing his horses because I'd put on a few pounds. And I get that. I'm supposed to stay lean and trim for races and such. But, he was just such a pompous, arrogant prick about it and things escalated, and before I knew it, I was telling him, 'I quit.'"

I expected him to respond. To say something, or chastise me, or warn me about the dangers of sleeping with my boss or some shit. But instead, I saw something boiling behind his eyes. A fury I'd never seen on any man's face before. I wasn't sure why, or what he was thinking about, but I knew better than to stay on topic.

So, I switched it quickly.

"How are you doing with things, though? Am I supposed to be hearing from your wife anytime soon about coming to see Marie Lee?"

He blinked, and the anger morphed into sadness. "Probably not."

I nodded slowly. "Do you want to talk about it?"

He leaned against the couch cushions, seemingly defeated. "What's there to talk about? I'm sure you already know what's happened. I mean, this town talks enough as it is. Everyone from here to the East Coast probably knows what's happening in my life right now."

I giggled. "I wouldn't go that far. But, at least the surrounding states, sure."

He chuckled. "What a shit-show I've got going on."

"If you want to talk about it, I'm all ears."

"Well, for starters, she's my ex-wife. I got served with divorce papers she's already had drawn up and signed."

My jaw dropped open. "When did this happen?"

"This afternoon. It's why I came home early."

"My God, Bryce. I'm so sorry. Have you gotten a chance to read them?"

He shook his head. "I'll read them once I settle in bed for the night."

"Well, you can use me for a distraction as long as you'd like."

I didn't clock the words that came out of my mouth. But, as his eyes held mine, something fell over his stare. And I'd been with enough men to know what that look was. I felt my nipples pucker against my bra. I felt my thighs tighten with want. I couldn't feel that way. It would be disastrous for everyone involved. I couldn't help it, though, especially with that carnal lust roiling in his brooding stare.

Say something. Anything. "How did you two meet?"

Bryce blinked. "What?"

I drew in a sobering breath. "You and your wife."

"Ex-wife."

"Right. How did you two meet?"

He blinked a few times before responding. "I met her at a party, and I took her back to the studio apartment I was renting at the time. We were a one-night stand until she knocked on my door a few weeks later, proclaiming that she was pregnant."

"Ah."

"We tried to go on a few dates, but the worry clouded both of our judgments. I wanted to do right by her and by the child we had created together, so when she was around three months pregnant, I proposed and we got married."

"You did that for her?"

He nodded slowly. "I told her I'd give her everything she needed. Her, and our child. And I figured that was that."

"I can't believe you did that for a woman you hardly knew."

He shrugged. "She was carrying my child. My daughter. I wanted to make sure the mother of my child was taken care of."

I couldn't believe what I was hearing. What a giving,

loving, sacrificial soul this man was. And she just up and left him? Like that?

Bryce sighed. "Anyway, I see your wine glass is a bit empty. Would you like some more?"

I smiled. "I'd love some, actually."

He stood. "Great. I'll go get the bottle because I could use one myself."

We sat there through three glasses of wine and kept talking. We pulled away from our exes and talked about our childhoods. Where we grew up. What our lives were like. We talked about dreams and life goals and family drama that always popped up. He talked to me about what it was like running that petroleum company with his brothers and how his parents seemed to be at a different beach in a different country every time they talked. I loved listening to him talk about his life. I adored watching his eyes light up as he talked about things he was passionate about.

And I enjoyed how he listened to me. Never once interrupting me, unless it was for clarification.

Dr. Morris had no issues running me over mid-sentence. Hell, most of the men I tried dating didn't have an ounce of interest in anything I had to say. Not Bryce, though. Bryce was different.

I liked that he was different.

Starlight poured through the windows as we laughed and talked. The minutes turned into hours as our bodies grew closer on the couch. At one point in time, he pulled my leg into his lap as I leaned back. Getting comfortable as he told me the story of the first time he ever heard Marie Lee laugh.

But then, he stopped talking. And the silence that hung around us was deafening.

"Bryce?" I asked.

I slowly sat up and saw him eyeing me heavily.

"Bryce?" I asked again.

His hand settled against my thigh. "Can I tell you something?"

I held myself up on my elbows. "Of course. You can tell me anything."

He squeezed my thigh softly. "You've been such a blessing to my daughter and me."

I smiled. "I'm glad I can help out."

"You're not just helping, though. You're improving. You're soaring, Willow. I mean, I've never seen my daughter act the way she does with you. I've never seen her take to someone like she has you."

"It's just my job. And she's a great kid. Just a bit lost, is all. But, kids are strong. They're more resilient than adults, that's for sure. She's going to be okay through all of this, you don't have to worry about that. Okay?"

I expected him to nod or agree with me. But instead, he leaned toward me. He pressed up onto his knees as my body seemingly lifted itself, meeting him halfway in midair. I felt my arms trembling. I felt my legs heating up. I watched his beautiful baby blue eyes come closer to me before he reached his hand out, brushing a strand of hair away from my cheek.

One that tickled my eye and caused it to water.

"There we go. That probably feels better," he said.

I tried not to feel disappointed. "No telling how long that's been there."

He smiled softly. "You've got another one right... here."

I felt my lip twitch as he slid another piece of hair away from my face that had gotten stuck somewhere it shouldn't be. And when his lingering touch warmed my skin, a shiver worked its way down my spine. I couldn't take my eyes off him. I didn't want the moment to end. I felt my waist flare up with heat at the memory of his muscles against my body and I wanted nothing more than to pull him against me and kiss him senseless.

I resisted the urge, though.

However, he didn't.

And before I could blink, his lips were against mine as I tugged his body down on top of me. Our glasses of wine, completely ignored as they tumbled to the floor.

12

Bryce

The second her curves caught my fall, I was lost in her. The feel of her pillowy lips against my own was something I'd never felt in my entire life. My hands cupped her clothed breasts as her legs spread for me, the couch cushions trying to make way for our debauchery. And as I felt her nipples puckering against her bra, the only thing I could think about was getting her out of it.

So I could see those amazing tits for myself.

Our clothes came off in a fury as we tumbled to the floor. I smelled wine soaking into my pristine brown carpet, but I didn't give a shit. I sucked on her lower lip and listened to the lovely moan that bubbled up the back of her throat. I felt the heat of her pussy radiating against my cock as I stiffened just for her. The meat of her inner thigh cradled my throbbing girth, my tip leaking with a need for her. And as her back arched, pressing her tits against my chest, my lips slid down her neck.

"Oh, Bryce."

That soft whisper of adoration sent me into a feeding frenzy. I wiggled myself between her legs, admiring the glistening of her pussy lips. I wanted all of her. I wanted to taste her, and fuck her, and feel her riding my cock. And tonight, I'd get all of it.

And so much more.

I growled as my tongue pierced her lower lips. Her legs slid over my shoulders as I cradled her, taking her hands within mine. I pulled her hands toward me, arching her back for my viewing pleasure. And as I lapped at her clit deeply, her chest bounced for me. Her skin flushed for me. Her moans filled my ears as if I were the only person on the planet along with her.

I enjoyed every millisecond of it.

"Bryce. Oh, fuck. Right there. So good. That's so good. You're so good. Oh, shit. I'm gonna come. I'm gonna come. I'm gonna--."

I didn't stop drinking her down until every fiber of her began shuddering for me. I pressed my tongue heavily against her clit, feeling her bucking ravenously. I let her use me. I let her coat my cheeks in her juices. And as they poured into my mouth, I swallowed every drop of her whole. My cock ached against the soft carpet. Her back collapsed against the floor. I rushed up her body, kissing and sucking. Licking and marking until our eyes connected, and my cock seated itself at her entrance.

And when her arms threaded around my neck, she pulled my lips down to hers.

I slid inside her with one fateful thrust, swallowing her sounds while she swallowed my own. Every single hair on my body stood on end as I thrust inside her, feeling her walls already massaging me. They swelled around me, urging my cock to grow. Urging me to move faster. And as my hips pounded against hers, I felt the whole of her excess jumping against me.

Filling me with a pride, I'd never experienced in all my life.

"Oh, fuck," I growled.

She locked her legs around my waist. "That's it. Don't stop. Don't stop, Bryce. Oh, shit."

Her wetness dripped down my balls. "Damn it, Willow. What the hell have you done to me?"

I felt my inner beast rattling around in its cage. I worked to keep it at bay, to keep my movements even and steady. But, all I wanted to do was pick her up, press her into a wall, and fuck her until she begged me to stop.

Maybe another time.

"Bryce!"

I grunted. "So. Close."

Her nails raked against my back before she stilled, her body shivering beneath me. Her pussy quickened around my cock, sucking me dry as my balls pulled into my body. I felt my hips shuttering. I felt my body caving. And as thread after thread of hot arousal shot from my tip, I collapsed against her.

Sucking my mark against her shoulder as I filled her to the brim.

The world swirled around me as she milked me dry. I buried my face into the crook of her neck as she laid there, splayed out for my viewing pleasure. Her whimpers and sighs filled my ears, reminding me of the pleasure we had just experienced. Reminding me that this wasn't a dream. That this was real.

That she really just let me have her.

"Willow," I murmured.

All she could do was whimper softly as I kissed her neck.

"Are you all right?" I whispered.

She giggled softly. "Oh, yeah."

I grinned. "Good."

I finally slid out from between her legs and rolled off to the side. I laid there, my arm against her stomach, as the two of us panted for air. I was covered in sweat, but whose sweat? I didn't know. Whether it was mine or hers, it didn't matter. The only thing that mattered was the heady feeling swirling around inside my skull.

Was this what sex felt like for every other adult?

Because I sure as hell had never experienced this before.

I closed my eyes and let the world tilt. I let my body roll along for the ride as my hand softly searched for hers. I wanted to hold her close. I wanted to cradle her in my arms. I wanted to lay there until we were both ready for a second round before throwing her over my shoulder and taking her out to that hot tub. I could see it already: her skin puckering from the heat—her clit, exposed to the jets, making her jump with delight as I filled her asshole. I could already taste her again, her legs spread as her naked body sat on the edge of that tub. Her head back, crying out for more while the acres of my empty estate swallowed her luscious sounds whole.

"Willow, that was--."

I felt her body moving quickly before the sound of a sniffle hit my ears. And when I lobbed my head off to the side, I watched Willow scramble for her clothes. I furrowed my brow tightly as I propped myself up, watching her cling tightly to the clothes that I had scattered all over the carpet of my living room. And then, I heard it again.

That telltale sniffle.

"Willow, what's wrong?" I asked.

She didn't answer me, though. All she did was make a break for the back patio doors, naked as a fucking jaybird. I pushed myself up onto my feet, trying to catch her before she dashed out into the darkness without a single bit of clothes on. And as worry pooled in my gut, I couldn't even steady myself onto my feet before she rushed out into the night.

"Willow!" I exclaimed.

I stumbled over to the open doors on my wobbling legs, painfully aware of the fact that I was naked and standing out on the porch. I watched as Willow tore across the lawn, walking around the pool before she sought out the comfort of that guesthouse I had. I watched her charge through the door and slam it behind her. I watched her shadow move quickly behind the windows before even the movement of her body fled from my sight.

And as I stood there, shocked and awed at the same time, the sounds of her sniffling echoed off the corners of my mind.

Willow had been crying. After having sex with me.

Had I forced her into something she didn't want?

The thought shivered me to my core as I forced myself to go back inside.

I slid the door closed and pulled the blinds before looking behind me at the mess we made. Her womanly scent still hung heavily in the room as my eyes fell upon the wine stains on my carpet. I cursed lowly to myself as I marched into the kitchen, digging out the cleaning supplies Maria kept firmly stocked in this place. And as I grabbed some paper towels, I drew in a deep breath. I'd have to talk with Willow tomorrow to make sure she was all right. To make sure I hadn't forced her into something she felt she had to do in order to keep her damn job.

But until then, I resisted the urge to put on my clothes and follow her.

Because my body still wanted to be laying there against hers.

13

Willow

I sat there, rubbing Marie Lee's back as I stared off at the wall. I had taken great strides to avoid Bryce all morning until he went off to work. But, I noticed that he had been late getting to work. Clearly, he wanted to speak with me. To catch me after what happened last night. But, I wasn't ready to address it. I wasn't ready to talk about it. So, I avoided him at all costs, using my job and his daughter as an excuse to leave him in the dust.

For now, at least.

"Hush little Marie, don't say a word," I sang softly.

I wasn't sure how many times I'd sung through that song, but I did it one last time for good measure. I wanted to make sure Marie Lee was good and asleep before I made my way back downstairs. She knew something was off. She kept giving me these looks every time I deviated away from the schedule I set for us. She tried to keep me on schedule, too, by asking me questions and pointing at things we should've been doing. Like, the bookshelf of books I had made for her. Or, the kitchen when snack time rolled around, where her father was standing conveniently snacking on some cherry grapes. It was as if the two of them were conspiring against me, and I wouldn't allow it.

But, once the song ended, and Marie Lee's light snores filled the room, I quickly made my leave.

I called Sadie and Luna as I flopped down in the library room at the front of the house.

"Girl!" Sadie exclaimed when she picked up the phone, "I never thought I'd hear from you again."

Luna giggled. "Yeah, we haven't even so much as heard your voice since you moved in."

Sadie interjected. "How's the job? How's Bryce doing?"

I heard Luna's grin through the phone. "You still staring at the hunk of man meat you're around all the time?"

And when I sighed, I knew they both heard the stress in my voice.

"Uh oh," Sadie murmured.

Luna paused. "Something wrong with the job?"

I pinched the bridge of my nose. "I slept with Bryce last night."

I expected a lot of things to happen in that moment. I expected them to scream, either with excitement or with anger. I expected Sadie to want all of the details while trying to tell Luna how things led up to that point. But instead, what I got was silence.

And it was unnerving.

"You guys there?" I asked warily.

Sadie was the first to speak. "I'm sorry, you what?"

Luna coughed. "You... slept with Bryce?"

Sadie scoffed. "You slept with your boss? Again?"

I slumped in the chair I was sitting in. "I know, I know."

Sadie sighed. "Did we not learn the first time this happened?"

I cleared my throat. "It's so much more complicated than-_."

"How did the hell did this even happen?" Luna asked.

My eyes flew open. "Did you just...?"

Sadie snickered. "She's so shocked that you've got her cussing. You hear that?"

I shook my head. "I feel like a child about to be grounded for the rest of her life."

Sadie giggled bitterly. "As you should be! Did you learn nothing from Dr. Morris?"

I licked my lips. "He's not like Dr. Morris. Nowhere in the realm of the same kind of thing."

Luna muttered. "He's your boss, and that's really all that matters in this situation right now."

"As much as I hate to admit it, she's right. You know I'm a sucker for a nice raunchy story, but now you have a pattern that isn't healthy in your life. We have to address it," Sadie said.

I scoffed. "Trust me, I feel shitty enough."

I heard Sadie flop onto her squeaky couch. "So, how the hell did this happen? I mean, we were there--what?--a a couple of weekends ago? And things felt completely platonic between you too."

Luna giggled. "Minus the drooling we were all doing. He is pretty tasty."

I furrowed my brow. "What have I entered, the twilight zone?"

Sadie ignored my comment. "How did this come about?"

I stared out the window. "I don't know, really. It just... happened."

Luna spoke softly. "Like it just happened with Dr. Morris?"

I didn't say anything because she had a point. Just like I'd practically thrown myself at him, I'd thrown myself at Bryce. Staring too much. Making any excuse to be in his presence. Allowing him to get much too close after having too much wine with him last night. It was so much like my situation with Dr. Morris. It was uncanny.

I can't be his full-time nanny. Not like this.

Sadie's voice pierced my thoughts. "Earth to Willow. You there?"

Luna hissed. "Just give her a minute, would you?"

I cleared my throat. "Sorry. I'm here. Just got a lot on my mind."

Sadie giggled. "Like that man and his muscles?"

I suppressed a groan. "No. Like, how I need another job."

Luna balked. "What!?"

Sadie sighed. "Oh, come on. Give yourself a little more credit than that. You can't just go around quitting your jobs because you have a slip-up with the boss."

I stood to my feet. "No, no. I need to quit. I need to get Marie Lee and Bryce on their feet after all this nonsense they've been through, then I need to help them find a replacement."

"And why do you feel that way, exactly?" Luna asked.

I drew in a sobering breath. "Because I know the longer I stay, the more of a chance there is that it'll happen again."

Sadie sighed. "It doesn't have to be this way."

"It really doesn't," Luna said with confidence, "we know how much you love children, and how much you love to help people, in general. This is the perfect job for you. Don't let one little mistake--."

My voice grew bitter. "This isn't a little mistake, Luna. I slept with my boss. Again. And I know damn good, and well it'll happen again if I allow it to. If I get myself alone with him again. I can't let that happen. That man, and his daughter, are going through enough. The last thing they need is some half-assed nanny making things even harder by throwing her body around."

"Now you wait just a second," Sadie said harshly. "You know damn good, and well, this is just as much his fault as it is yours. I mean, I don't know what happened or anything, but I know you better than that. I know you didn't throw yourself at him. In fact, I'd be willing to bet my soul he probably made the first move, and you just went along with things, and now you're feeling guilty that you didn't stop him. Right?"

I paused. "I don't know. I really don't."

Luna jumped in. "And that's fine. It's okay that you don't know. But, I don't think the right conclusion is to automatically assume you can't do this job."

I marched out of the room. "I've already made up my mind. Once I get them back on their feet and get things normal around here, I have to find a replacement. I have to find another job. I've done a terrible thing--."

"Hey, he's a party in this, too," Sadie said.

I suppressed my angry tone. "*We've* done a terrible thing. And it's only going to get worse as time goes on. Either it's going to make things awkward, or it's going to bring about emotions no one needs right now."

Luna cleared her throat. "Willow--."

I didn't let her get started. "You guys said it yourself. I've made this a trend now—an ugly, nasty, good-for-nothing trend. And I can't continue like this. I have to cut this off at the head before it grows into something like what I had with Dr. Morris. We both deserve better than that. Bryce deserves better, and so do I. I don't want to be this person, you guys. I don't want to be 'that girl'."

Sadie's voice grew soft. "You could never be 'that girl', Willow. Not with how much you love."

My eyes watered over. "I just need a job where I work and do the right things. That's what I need in my life right now.

Whether it comes with racing or not, I don't even care. But, I know this isn't the right place for me. It never was, and it never will be. I can't do wrong by this man not just because of what he's going through, but because he's got an innocent daughter in the mix."

Luna sighed. "Is there anything we can do to talk you out of it?"

I wish. "No."

The phone fell silent for a while before Sadie spoke up.

"Then, we support you in whatever you decide to do."

"Yeah," Luna said, "we're with you, whatever you need."

I walked into the kitchen. "Thanks, guys. I appreciate it."

After winding things down and hanging up the phone with my two best friends, I gazed out the kitchen window. I conjured the memory of Bryce swimming in the pool that night, with the moon igniting his body in ways I'd never seen before. I pressed my hand softly against the kitchen window glass. I watched the phantom memory of his almost-naked body swimming back and forth in the clear, pristine, undisturbed pool. How a man could be so beautiful, yet so deadly, I'd never know. But, as I turned toward the living room, the memory of him was everywhere.

I saw him dancing with his daughter and smiling as he held me in his arms. I saw the ghost of our bodies tumbling to the floor from the couch, writhing and grinding like two mad people, trying to forget their pasts. A tear trickled down my cheek before I quickly wiped it away. I thought about all the pain he must be in. All the pain Marie Lee must feel on a daily basis. And I cursed his wife--well, almost-ex-wife--for what she'd done to them. She was an absolute idiot to leave all of this behind. And if she thought she'd somehow find something better than this, she was sorely mistaken.

Because this was as good as life got.

But it wasn't my life to enjoy.

"You're such an idiot," I whispered to myself.

With the baby monitor in my hand, I made my way out back. I forced the memories away as I sprinted for the guest house, reaching for the only place his presence hadn't defiled yet. I slammed through the door and closed it behind me, eyeing my laptop heavily. And as I walked over to the small breakfast nook this place afforded me, I braced myself for the job hunt.

I knew that with every minute I stayed, I'd convince myself that I could have this kind of life. That I could swoop in, replace his ex-wife, and all would be well. I knew that if I stayed, I'd convince myself that he wanted me there. That he needed me there, as much for him as for his daughter. I'd paint this lovely picture in my mind of something that wasn't unfolding because I was nothing but lonely.

Lonely, depressed, and useless.

"Fucking hell," I hissed.

Bryce was a stand-up man who stood by a woman he got pregnant, and he deserved a stand-up woman. Not some woman who slept with her bosses in exchange for racing their horses. My fingers clicked across the keyboard as I ignored my faint reflection in the laptop screen. When in the world had I become this person? When did I go from a strong, dreaming woman with a college education to a weak-willed college girl that threw herself at every successful man that crossed her path?

Bryce deserved better. His daughter deserved better. And that meant I had to leave.

Even if I was already falling in love with him and his daughter.

14

Bryce

My phone rang, and I sighed as I answered it. "This is Bryce."

"Mr. Remington. It's Detective Peterson."

My back stiffened, feeling the stress immediately come over me. "Detective. I wasn't sure I'd ever hear from you again."

He chuckled dryly as if he had heard that multiple times through his career. "Well, jobs like this usually just take time. The first couple of weeks is all about learning her movements...where she goes on a regular basis...who I can expect to see her with regularly. Then, it's all about picking those places apart for answers as to why she goes."

I blinked. "Right. So, uh, you got anything for me?"

"I wanted to call because I've pulled some phone records to take a look at. You know, match those numbers with the people I see her with on a regular basis. And she's got a great deal of phone calls going to and from a burner number. A few different ones, in fact."

"Burner phones? You think she's in some kind of trouble?" I wanted to be worried about her, but that was very difficult for me.

"On the contrary, actually. I think the burner phones connect us to the man you say your wife left you for. Because these numbers predate the day that you told me she walked out."

My jaw clenched, and my hand curled into a ball. "She was receiving calls from some burner phone asshole even while she was still in the house?"

"I could only pull her records so far back. But, I've got the past six months' worth of records, and these numbers are strewn throughout the days. I've got in a queue to pull text messages as well, but that takes infinitely more time to get my hands on."

I swallowed down a growl. "Call me the second you do."

"Noted. But, there's something else you need to be aware of. I stumbled upon it after listening to a very juicy conversation between her and a 'Miss Lila Edwards.' That name ring a bell?"

I scoffed, rolling my eyes. "Lila's her best friend. Why?"

"Well, they were having coffee about a week ago together, and Lila mentioned something about funds. Your wife--."

"Ex-wife."

"Right. Your ex-wife got pretty uneasy about the conversation. She switched over to talking about something else, so I did some digging. Turns out, she's got a bank account in an Auston bank in her maiden name."

I blinked. "Her maiden name?"

"Yes, sir. Took me a while to pull the records, but once I did, I noticed a trend. Twice a month, on the nose with the days, there are regular deposits that always equal two-thousand dollars that go into this Auston account. And it didn't take long to trace back where that money is coming from."

I sighed. "You gotta be kidding me."

"I'm afraid not, Mr. Remington. She's been siphoning money out of your joint accounts. You know, a little bit here and there from each account that total up to two-thousand dollars and putting it in this personal account of hers for a while now. It would make it hard for someone to notice unless they were specifically looking for something since the deposits are not always the same... but always equal two-thousand bucks."

I dreaded the answer to my question. "How long?"

He shuffled his papers and cleared his throat uncomfortably. "You said you two have been together for about two years, right?"

I growled at him. "How long, detective."

He paused. "The payments started about two years ago, Mr. Remington."

It felt like a knife had been driven into my heart. For a

split second, I couldn't even breathe. My wife. The mother of my child. Siphoning money off me from the beginning? Had that been her plan all along? Did our marriage not have anything to do with starting our family together? I had done right by her. Made an honest woman out of her so this community she proclaimed to love wouldn't look down their noses at her as an unwedded mother. And she does this to me?

Did she ever care for me?

Was the plan all along to get my money and run?

"Sir, do you want me to--?"

I drew in a deep breath through my nose. "Yes. I want you to compile the information and get it over to me, please."

"I can do that. In the meantime, is there anything else you want me to pursue? Now that I've read you in?"

I snickered. 'Read me in,' like we were pursuing some sort of high-level fugitive. "Not for now. Just stick with figuring out who the hell this man is that she's run off with. I'd like to know the face of the person that's keeping my daughter's mother away from her."

"Of course, Mr. Remington."

"In the meantime, get me all of that information as quickly as you can. We'll talk soon."

"I'll get it to you by tomorrow morning at the latest."

I pinched the bridge of my nose. "Thanks."

The second I hung up the phone, my eyes fell to the calculator sitting next to my computer. Did I dare? I mean, the math was easy enough to do in my head. But, did I dare type it out and stare at it? Looking at it might make it all the more real. It might just send me over the edge.

It was as if I couldn't help but hurt myself further.

"Two thousand twice is four grand. So, four grand times twelve..."

Forty-eight grand.

"And that times two..."

Just shy of one hundred grand.

I stared down at the number in shock. That was ninety-six thousand dollars over the course of two years. On the one hand, if I could go two years without noticing four grand disappearing from my accounts each month, then it meant I was doing much better in my career than I had figured. And besides I trusted her and never thought about double-checking our joint bank accounts. Staring down at that number made me sick, and I was grateful her name wasn't on any of the Remington family's business accounts.

I shook my head, wondering if this was the small price she was willing to pay for sacrificing her life with her daughter? Ninety-six grand and some guy that fucked her better in bed? It made me want to cry out in pain...in horror...in disgust...at the sins that had been committed against Marie Lee. All this time and that woman still hadn't managed to find the time to come up for air and even text me asking about our daughter.

Yet here she was. Living high off my dime.

"She doesn't get a cent more," I murmured.

As I scrambled around for the divorce papers I still hadn't looked at, a burst of bitter laughter fell from my lips. How in the world could I have been so damn stupid? I mean, I'd funded everything for this woman. Her shopping trips, paying off her credit cards every month, and pretty much anything else she desired. And here she had been, siphoning yet more money off me like some common jezebel; siphoning money so she could abandon the only two people in her corner someday to run off with a common bull in a suit.

This guy must really be a piece of work.

I laid my hands on that manilla envelope and decided to kickback. I slid the stack of papers out and actually started reading them. Something I hadn't dared do since I was first served by that assistant in a terrible suit coat. And what I found was nearly highway robbery.

"Half? Of everything!?" I exclaimed.

I bolted upright, almost knocking my computer over as I slid my legs off my damn desk. My eyes bulged as I looked down at the list of things and demands Patricia had before she'd settle this divorce. My eyes kept widening with every word I read. She wanted alimony, a massive amount of child support--which I was fine with--and on top of that? Half of my retirement. My investments. My savings accounts.

All in all, she was asking for a settlement totaling several million bucks.

And that was just the first payout.

"Oh, hell no," I murmured.

I picked up my phone and instantly dialed my family company's lawyer.

"Mr. Remington. How can I help--?"

I cut her off. "I need the number to a very, very good divorce lawyer."

Mrs. Jenkins paused. "I happen to know the best divorce lawyer in this part of the country."

"Pay whatever he or she requires for their fees. Because my divorce isn't going down like my ex thinks it's about to."

"Care to read me in on some of the facts? That way, I know how to present this to *him*, by the way. His name is DaShawn Abbott."

I nodded. "Wonderful. Well, for starters, I just figured out via a private investigator that my ex-wife has siphoned money from our joint accounts into a personal one to the tune of almost a hundred grand. She left me high and dry with Marie Lee to galavant off with some young stud--which I have proof of with the note she left behind--, and now she's sent me divorce papers. She's asking for half of everything, including my retirement accounts, after she left me for another man and hasn't once checked up on her daughter."

I heard her scribbling in the background. "Custody agreement?"

"I want Marie Lee. Plain and simple."

"Right. What's the child support payment a month she has laid out."

I chuckled bitterly. "Four grand. Which happens to be the exact amount of money she's been siphoning off me every month for the past two damn years."

Her voice fell flat. "How convenient. All right, I have what

I need. I'll give DaShawn a call right now, and if he has room in his schedule, I'll pass on your information."

"Tell him I'll pay him double if he makes the time."

"Done, and done. Keep your phone close, Mr. Remington."

I sighed with relief. "Thank you, ma'am."

My company's lawyer hung up the phone, and I tossed everything onto my desk. The divorce papers, my cell phone, and a bit of my pride as well. I ran my hands down my face before I leaned back, staring up at the ceiling. And as I sat there, I noticed something.

I wasn't heartbroken.

The betrayal hurt, yes. And the loss of the money was really not an issue. I hurt for Marie Lee, though. My daughter had lost her mother and had no clue why. But, was I sad at Patricia leaving me? Leaving us?

Not in the slightest.

"Well then," I whispered.

Suddenly, a wondrous sound cascaded against my ears. I grinned at the girlish giggles and squeals that came from the backyard. I stood to my feet, stretching my arms above my head as I made my way over to the window. And as my back popped a million times straight into place, I peered down at Marie Lee. At my daughter, with her beautiful ringlet curls, running around the backyard with Willow chasing her. The two of them looked to be having the grandest time together, and my heart warmed at the sight.

Willow had been a godsend for both of us.

I walked over to the bay window and sat in the sill, watching them play down below. Willow scooped my daughter into her arms and started twirling around as if she had caught some sort of magic treasure. Which only made my daughter laugh harder. The sound tugged a smile across my cheeks. It set a fire ablaze in my gut, and it made me wonder if Willow was as happy here as we were to have her here.

As *I* was to have her here.

I saw Willow bringing my daughter into the house, so I made my way downstairs. I enjoyed the privacy of my home office, but sometimes being at home was a great distraction, especially with Willow around. Recently, I definitely was more focused at our family's business office near the stables. Still, she and I needed to talk. My confrontations for the day weren't over, and I needed to make sure I utilized my daughter's nap time well.

Willow and I still had yet to talk about our encounter a little while back.

"Anyone ready for some lunch?" I called out as I came down the stairs.

"Daddy!" Marie Lee exclaimed.

I held out my arms. "Come here, princess."

She jumped down from Willow's hip and dashed into my arms. I hugged her tightly and picked her up, swinging her around just to hear that giggle in my ear again. I peppered her cheek with kisses. I felt her small arms clinging to me around my neck. But, when I lifted my eyes to look at Willow, I saw nothing but hesitancy and regret staring back at me in hers.

It killed me to see it because I knew it was about the night we shared. I felt nothing but joy and ecstasy. However, she was filled with nothing but regret and worry.

We really needed to talk today.

"Looks like someone's already tired," Willow finally said.

She nodded to Marie Lee, who had already fallen asleep on my shoulder.

"Should we wake her up to eat?" I asked softly.

She shook her head, walking towards me. "No. She can eat once she's up. Here. I'll go put her down."

"Will you eat lunch with me, then?"

Her eyes flashed to me, momentarily as she scooped Marie Lee from my arms. And the look in her eye told me she didn't want to talk. Hell, her body language told me she didn't want to be within a few feet of me, but that didn't stop me from wanting to be around her.

"I've actually got some chores I need to do around here," Willow whispered.

"You know you don't actually have to clean, right? That's what Maria is here for."

She shrugged, making her way toward the stairs. "I still like to clean up a bit. I mean, she's not responsible for the backyard, and we've made a pretty good mess out there."

"Well, then how about tonight?"

"I'm not sure, Bryce..."

"Please?"

She stopped in her tracks and looked down at me from halfway up the stairs. I'd plead with her if that's what it took because I didn't want this weirdness between us. I didn't want this awkwardness to create distance when she was so good for our family. I gazed into her eyes as my soul pleaded with hers. Hell, I would've gotten on my knees if I would've thought it might make a difference.

"Please, Willow. Can we talk tonight? Maybe after dinner? No wine, I promise."

Then finally, she nodded. "Sure. We can talk then."

I clasped my hands together. "Thank you. Really."

"You're welcome. Now, let me go get her down."

"Of course. Yeah, yeah, you go, and I'll," I snickered, "see you tonight." Smiling, I watched as she made her way up the rest of the stairs.

Only to disappear down the hallway above my head.

15

Willow

"Hello there, sweet girl," I said with a smile on my face.

Marie Lee stretched her arms over her head before turning over onto her side. So, I started rubbing her back.

"Oh, no-no. You gotta get up, pretty girl."

She pulled the covers over her head as an answer to my statement, and it made me laugh.

"All right, you lazy butt. Come on. Nap time's over."

I scooped a limp Willow out of her bed as she groaned. Her head fell against my shoulder before she clung to me, and my heart skipped a beat. Every time this wondrous little girl reached for me or took my hand or wrapped her arms around my neck, I couldn't help but love her all the more. She was precious as they came, and it sickened me that someone would be idiotic enough to abandon her.

To abandon both of them.

I walked a sleepy Marie Lee downstairs and started the back half of our routine. I sat her down at the table in her booster chair and set a small plate of healthy snacks in front of her. And if she wanted more since she slept through lunch, she could always get more. I got myself a cup of cool coffee and sat next to her, watching the sleepy girl pick at the fruits on her plate. Then, she looked over at me with those big baby doe eyes of hers and jutted out that lower lip.

"More?" she asked.

I booped her nose with my fingertip. "More, what?"

"More fruit?"

"More fruit, what?"

I saw the cogs in her head, turning. "Pwease?"

I smiled. "Of course, you can have more fruit."

After our power snack-slash-overdue-lunch, I wiped her down and took her into the living room. We sat in a small corner I had made up just for her of books and noise-free toys and things she could color on. We sat on the fluffy rug, and she chose the activity we'd do for the next hour, and when I saw her reach for the stenciling pad, I went ahead and started digging out the markers.

And for an hour, we doodled.

We drew stars and worked on the names of shapes. I helped her trace numbers, and we counted all the way to ten. She was smart for a little two-year-old. She had dexterity capabilities well beyond her age. And while she had various speech impediments that we were working on, that was the only outward sign that she was delayed in any sort of way.

In every other area of her life, she flourished.

"Good girl!" I praised after she accurately traced the number '3.'

When she smiled up at me with that gigantic wide smile of hers, my heart melted all over again.

"You'll be the death of me," I said with mock sternness on my face.

That made Marie Lee giggle profusely.

"You ready for exercise time?" I asked.

Her eyes lit up. "Swim?"

I peered over my shoulder. "Bright blue sky. Sun, unimpeded by clouds. I think we can go swimming for sure."

She hopped up. "Yay! Swim! Fwoaties, pwease!"

My head fell back with laughter. "Come on. Let's get into your bathing suit."

After exercising for an hour in the pool and enjoying a popsicle while drying off in the sun, it was time for our free hour. For one hour a day, Marie Lee got to do whatever she wanted, leading up to the preparations for dinner. And today, she wanted to swing on the porch swing out front. She tugged her Peppa Pig blanket behind her and crawled up onto the swinging piece of finished wood, waiting for me to join her. So, with a drink for each of us, I headed out front and sat down with her, the swing softly swaying in the summer breeze that kicked up.

And as she crooked herself beneath my arm, resting her head against my bosom, a daring thought crossed my mind.

This is all I want in life.

I blinked back tears as the words rattled around in my head. The talk that was coming with Bryce wouldn't be good, that much was for certain. And here I was, reaping the benefits of a life I didn't deserve while taking care of a little girl that could never be mine. It made me angry for many reasons. It made me mad that I'd never have something as beautiful as this. It made me mad that there were selfish, spoiled women out there with options to simply run away from all this. It made me angry that Bryce and Marie Lee were left high and dry without any explanation. Yet, I was here to help pick up the pieces of that fallout without any explanations myself. All of it seemed so unfair and so cruel.

Especially when Bryce was on the brink of firing me.

Our interactions this afternoon gave me pause for my concerns. But, I was still of the mind that he was about to let me down as gently as he could. And for a good reason, too. Things were supposed to be stable around here for Marie Lee's benefit. That needed to be our only focus, and clearly, the only thing we could do was focus on one another. If it were my child? It would've been grounds enough for me to fire someone.

So, I soaked up every single moment I could with Marie

Lee and committed every wonderful emotion I had in the process to memory.

Because I wasn't sure I'd ever experience it again.

We swung on the porch swing until Bryce pulled up in the driveway. Then, Marie Lee hopped down and took off running towards her father. I stood as I watched him scoop her up and spin her around. I watched as she clung to her 'Daddy' tightly. I watched as the two of them gazed into each other's eyes, so far beyond in love that they didn't know what to do with themselves.

It kind of made me jealous.

And it reminded me of why I needed to accept my fate head-on tonight.

My work here is done.

Dinner was silent and awkward. Bryce tried to break the silence every now and again, but it didn't really work. I was suddenly too tired to give him full-on answers to his questions, and eventually, he stopped asking them. All too soon, however, dinner was over, and the bedtime routine was enacted.

And that's when he shocked me.

"Here, let me help you guys tonight," Bryce said.

I furrowed my brow. "We've got it, Mr. Remington. Just give me a few minutes, and I'll be down."

He winced. "Mr. Remington?"

Marie Lee giggled. "You mean, Daddy."

I grinned at her. "I'll be down in a bit, *Mr. Remington.*"

But, he started up the steps. "I won't take 'no' for an

answer. Now, come on. Show me this almighty bedtime routine we've got going on."

I sighed. "All right. I need you to take her into her bedroom so she can pick out a pair of pajamas. We won't bother with a bath tonight, but I am going to wipe her down with wipes and but some lotion on her, so her skin doesn't dry out."

Marie Lee took her father's hand. "Even on the feets?"

I grinned. "Even on your feet, yes, Marie Lee."

Bryce chuckled. "She's very ticklish on her feet."

I turned toward the bathroom. "Trust me, I've figured that out."

He barked with laughter, and I tried to stuff down how I was feeling. But, as Bryce helped me with his daughter's bedtime routine, it kind of felt like we were family. Him, holding Marie Lee still so I could lotion down her feet. Me, helping her into her pajamas while he loaded up her toothbrush with paste. The two of us, sitting on either side of her bed while I read the bedtime story she finally let me pick out for her. Even both of us sneaking out quietly so as to not disturb her after she'd fallen asleep.

It felt good.

Too good.

And it only reminded me of why I needed to get the hell out of there.

"So," I said as I made my way toward the stairs.

"So," Bryce repeated.

"You... wanted to talk?"

He held out his hand, ushering me down the stairs. "Let's get a glass of wine and chat."

I crooked an eyebrow. "Sure, wine is a smart choice of drink?"

He paused. "You got a point. Uh... sparkling cider?"

I smiled. "Sounds good to me."

"Great. Great. I'll go get us a glass and meet you on the couch."

"Maybe the kitchen table, instead?"

His eyes found mine as we came to the bottom of the steps. "Sure. Yeah. We can sit there, too."

I watched him curiously as he made his way into the kitchen. I could've sworn I heard disappointment in his voice, but I also wasn't sure. For all I knew, my mind was playing tricks on me. Trying to find the slightest bit of hope in this situation like the masochist it was. I shook my head and started for the kitchen table. Bryce set a glass of sparkling cider in front of me before taking a seat next to me. Not across from me, or at the head of the table. But, right next to me.

Where I could feel the warmth of his thigh against my own.

"So, I'm just going to blurt out what's on my mind and your rebuttal. Is that okay?" he asked.

I sipped my drink, trying not to look over at him. "Sure. Yeah."

He drew in a deep breath. "All right. Here goes. I'm sorry if I crossed a line last time we were together, and if I made you uncomfortable at all, I'm really sorry. I never meant to make you feel that way, and if I did, I'd like to make it up to you somehow."

His words pulled my eyes over to his. "Make it up to me?"

He nodded. "Yeah. Maybe with some time off? Or a sincere apology? Or, I could pay your race dues for the next few races."

"So, you want to bribe my silence."

"No! No, no, no. Nothing like that. I just--I--it's--."

I giggled. "Bryce, I'm just joking. It's okay."

He sighed with relief. "So, we're okay?"

I swallowed hard. "I don't know. Are we?"

He scooted closer. "I'd like to think we are."

Don't stare in his eyes. Don't stare in his eyes. "Yeah, we are."

He grinned. "Good. Because for a while now, I felt like maybe you only went along with what happened because I was your boss? And you didn't feel like you could say 'no'?"

His words shocked me to my core. "Let's get one thing straight, Bryce. You listening?"

"Yes, ma'am."

"Under no circumstances did you sway me into doing something I didn't want. I'm a grown woman, and I want what I want. And if I didn't want you that night, I would've made sure you understood. Got it?"

He nodded slowly. "Yes, ma'am."

I let out the breath I had been holding. "Is there anything else you wanna talk about?"

His eyes searched mine. "A lot."

My heart stopped in my chest. "Like... like what?"

I watched his hand raise up, and my eyes were captured by the movement. His fingertips gravitated toward my ear, and I froze, wondering what he'd do next. I needed to tell him to stop. I needed to tell him not to touch me. But damn it, I wanted that man's hands all over me.

And when he tucked a loose strand of hair behind my ear, my walls caved just that easily.

"Kiss me," I whispered.

His eyes fell to my lips. "Just kiss you?"

I reached out, gripping his shirt. "Do whatever you want to me."

I dragged his body against my own, knowing damn good and well I had no one to blame but myself. However, if I was only going to get a limited amount of time to be in Bryce's life like this, then why the hell shouldn't I take the opportunity? It was clear he wanted me. And I wanted him. If he was concerned enough about my well-being to have this kind of conversation only to apologize, then I knew he wouldn't screw me over in the end. We'd part ways once it was time with nothing but smiles. That, I was sure of.

So, with worries slowly sliding off my back, I purred at the moment Bryce wrapped his strong arms around me.

And hauled me out of that fucking chair.

"Come here, beautiful," he growled.

16

Bryce

The taste of her skin against my tongue sent me flying into the heavens. The way her thick curves comforted me as my body pressed against hers sent my gut flaming with desire. I wrapped my arms around her, pulling her toward me as her head fell back. And with her moans came my name, a sweet cry for more as my cock stiffened against her clothed body.

"Come with me," I growled.

I needed her. All of her. And come hell or high water, I'd get it.

Now that I knew she wanted me as well, though, I knew nothing would be standing in my way. I tugged her over toward the couch. Our couch, to be honest. And as we fell to the cushions we kept christening with our debaucheries, my tongue lapped at her pulse point.

Causing her to shiver beneath me.

"We should memorialize this couch, you know," Willow said breathlessly.

I hovered my lips over her clothed tit as my eyes slowly slid up to hers. And when I caught her gaze, it was filled with a playfulness that made me feel like a teenage boy again.

I chuckled. "I can christen it with you. How does that sound?"

She licked her lips. "Christen away, then."

Her beckoning to me lit a fire beneath my ass that curled my fists against her clothing. I ripped them off, feeling seams and stitches tearing as I cast them to the floor. Her hands worked quickly to get my shirt over my head. Both of us had to work to get my fucking belt off before she ripped it from the belt loops of my jeans. By the time we were done, we were exposed to one another.

Again.

And I loved every second of it.

"You're beautiful, you know that?" I asked.

She swallowed hard. "You think so?"

My eyes held hers. "I know so, Willow."

She held her arms out for me, and I eased myself down against her. With our bodies splayed out across the couch, I softly connected my lips to hers. She tasted like sparkling cider and a second chance. She smelled like honey and sex. Our tongues fell together in a symphony of lust and desire, and as my cock settled against her wet pussy, I already felt her juices dripping against my skin.

"I can't wait. I need you. Please," she begged.

And damn it, it was the sweetest sound I'd ever heard in my life.

One by one, I pinned her wrists above her head. I held them down with one hand as my other hand slipped between us, gripping the shaft of my dick. I slid my tip up and down her slit, gathering juices as they lubed me up. Her eyes, half-hooded with desire, watched me like a hawk. And as a grin spread across my face, I inched the tip of my dick inside her.

Which was enough to flutter her eyes closed.

"You like that?" I asked.

She gasped. "Don't stop."

I inched in a bit further. "Like that?"

She whimpered. "Please. Let me have you. Just this once."

I nuzzled her nose with mine. "Oh, it'll be much more than 'once,' beautiful. That, I can promise."

I slammed the rest of the way inside of her, and her back arched. My lips dropped down to her puckered peaks, lapping and sucking and nibbling as I drove myself into her. Fucking her and feeling her curves bouncing as her legs locked around me. I felt powerful whenever I was above her. I felt wanted whenever I was inside of her. But, nothing compared to when I heard her moaning out my name. Crying out for more, as if I were the only person that could give it to her.

That gave my life meaning.

And I didn't want it to ever go away.

"Fucking hell, Willow," I grunted.

Her hips rolled against me. "More. More, Bryce. Please. Bryce. Holy shit, Bryce!"

The couch moved with my movements, scraping across the carpet as I lost myself in her. I released her wrists, bracing myself against the couch as I hooked her legs against my arms. I folded her in half, watching her curves bunch up for me as her body jiggled for my viewing pleasure. And as I sucked on her nipples, rendering her motionless, I felt her pussy gripping my dick.

"Yes! Bryce!"

I growled. "Come for me, Willow. Do it."

"So close. So close. Please, please, please, please. Yes!"

I stuffed her full as she exploded, her juices dripping down my cock. I gnashed my teeth together, holding back my own orgasm as I watched pleasure wash over her features. Her eyes rolled back into her head. Her jaw, unhinged with silent ecstasy. Her hands wrapped around my forearms, digging into me as she held on for dear life. I swiveled my hips, causing her to gasp for air. Her thighs shook against me, undulating as their excess put on a show I never wanted to end.

I felt high on life whenever I was with her.

I wrapped my arms around her and scooped her up. She clung to me, her thickness blanketing me as I sat back on the couch. With my back against the upright cushions and my legs spread to accommodate my hanging balls, I sat her in my lap. Her pussy, planted firmly against my cock.

"Take your time," I whispered, placing a kiss against her cheek.

But, when she rose up, the tip of my cock caught against her entrance.

And she slid down my girth as if her body were made for the journey.

"Your turn," she murmured against my ear.

My eyes rolled back as she started to move. Her juices, pouring down my skin. Her hands, massaging my shoulders as she rolled against my cock. Her hips, swiveling. Her body, bucking. And soon, my hands fisted her waist and directed her movements. I wasn't far from my own end. The way she moved astounded me in ways I'd never experienced before. What we had was powerful. Carnal. More amazing than anything I'd ever had in my whole life.

That included what I had with Marie Lee's mother.

"Willow," I grunted.

"That's it. I'm so close. Come with me, Bryce. Please."

I rolled against her. "Just a bit more. Just like that. Don't stop, Willow. Don't stop."

Then, I felt that tightening in my gut finally release.

"I'm coming! Oh, shit. I'm coming, Willow."

She collapsed against me, whimpering. "Bryce, oh my God."

I wrapped my arms around her as our bodies trembled together. I felt my cock emptying inside of her, marking her in ways I wanted to for the rest of my life. I had no idea what the hell this woman had done to me, but I never wanted to let it go. She had invaded my life and turned it upside down, and I didn't want to put things right ever again.

"Oh, Willow," I whispered.

She trembled against me, her pussy milking my cock for everything it had. We groaned and grunted together, taking what we could from the other and giving back without ever asking. I peppered kisses along her shoulder. I watched goosebumps trickle down the expanse of her luscious back. I pressed my face into the crook of her neck, kissing and nibbling as her sighs turned to giggles.

And as our orgasms finally died down, we were covered in nothing but sweat.

"Holy shit," she whispered.

I chuckled. "Took the words right out of my mouth."

Her head settled against my shoulder. "I'm just gonna rest here for a second. Okay?"

I smiled. "Rest as much as you please."

My quaking hand reached for one of the few blankets on this couch we hadn't already ruined, and I fluttered it around us. I wrapped us up as my cock still sat inside Willow's beautiful warmth as if it had finally found its home. Every once in a while, her lips would pucker, and I'd feel the smallest, sweetest kiss imaginable against my skin. Every time she did it, my heart stopped in my chest. Every time she moved, I gripped her. Held her to me. Because I sure as hell wasn't ready to let her go. I wanted us to stay like this. I never wanted the moment to end. With her thick curves calling to my muscles and her body wrapped tightly around mine, I wanted to walk her upstairs and curl up in my bed with her.

I wanted to wake up to her.

And the only thing stopping me was my daughter. Marie Lee. I didn't want to ruin the relationship she had with her nanny. I didn't want to be selfish, because this was first and foremost, for her. I needed Willow to stick around and keep this place afloat. I needed her in my daughter's life. So, I had to take things slowly. Maybe ask her out on a date next time instead of just hitting her with shit after dinner.

She deserved much better from me if this was going to be a regular occurrence.

"Willow?" I asked softly.

"Hmm?" she hummed.

"Would you object to possibly having dinner with me sometime?"

She shook her head softly. "No. I wouldn't."

I paused. "You wouldn't object, or...?"

But, the next sound I heard wasn't a 'yes' or a 'no.' It wasn't a confirmation or a denial. It wasn't any sort of clarification to the stupid question I had asked in her vulnerable state.

The next sounds I heard were her soft snores.

And while it made me smile, it also left me with more questions than answers.

"Way to go, idiot," I murmured to myself.

17

Willow

As I peered out the window, sipping my cup of coffee, I watched Bryce leading Sky around the backyard with Marie Lee riding her bareback. He had given the mare to his daughter since Sky couldn't barrel race any more, and Marie Lee was learning how to hold the reins. After a moment of pleasure watching the two, my thoughts returned to the last thing I remembered from the previous night.

I had been laying my head against Bryce's shoulder, and when I woke up this morning, I was in my own bed. Still naked, but covered up and in my own bed. Had he carried me there? I mean, it was the only logical explanation. Unless I was sleepwalking last night or something.

"No, he carried me back," I murmured.

He didn't just do that, though. He turned off my phone and unplugged the alarm by my bed. And when I woke up this morning, I woke up to a note that told me I'd have the day off. My first day off since starting here with them, and for some reason, I didn't want to take that day.

I wanted to be outside, helping Bryce give Marie Lee her first riding lesson.

Still, I enjoyed my cup of coffee at eleven in the morning as I watched Bryce steady his daughter as she shrieked with joy when Sky started to trot. I loved how the sun ignited his already sun-kissed skin. I loved how he squinted out from under the brim of his Stetson in the bright Texas sun. And I absolutely adored the way he and his daughter smiled at one another.

It was the purest form of love I'd ever seen in my life.

Needless to say, however, things didn't go the way I wanted them to go last night. But, the upside to that was that we shared a beautiful and wondrous moment with one another that I'd always cherish. Hell, even thinking about it while I sipped my coffee left me breathless. And every time it crossed my mind, it made me smile.

He made me smile.

"You're gonna fuck this uuuuup," I singsonged to myself.

Maybe you don't have to leave.

I sighed as I closed my eyes. I wasn't sure if last night had dropped my guard or if I just wasn't awake enough yet, but my desires were coming back to the forefront of my mind.

Already, I was considering myself instead of what was good for Marie Lee, and I despised myself for it. I shut the guesthouse blinds and backed away from the window. I forced myself into my bedroom, away from the giggling and that damn sexy man in a Stetson..

I needed to keep my distance until I could get my head screwed back on straight.

Then again, the more I thought about last night, the more I thought about other things. Like, how great it felt to put Marie Lee to bed together. Or, how nice it always felt to share family dinners with them. It's a very domesticated feeling and one that I felt suited both of us last night. Cleaning up together. Doing the bedtime routine together. Talking together after the kiddo went to bed. I didn't want to leave all of that. I didn't want to leave the bond I had built with these two.

"I'm sorry, what?"

I heard Bryce's voice startlingly close to my bedroom, and it made me jump. But then, I heard him growl. I couldn't make out what he was saying, but he didn't sound happy. And it made me wonder where the hell Marie Lee and Sky had gotten off to.

I almost got up to go check on her, but Bryce's words caught my ear and rooted me to my bed.

Is he on the back patio of the guesthouse?

"If she thinks that, she's out of her fucking mind."

I placed my coffee down and walked over to the corner of my room to listen.

"Well, why don't you call her and ask her why she hasn't called. Yeah?"

I pressed my ear to the wall as I held my breath.

"No, you won't be hearing from me again until I have a lawyer myself. Goodbye."

My heart sank for him as I heard his boots against the tiled patio floor, lumbering away. I peeked out of my bedroom window, watching as his body finally emerged, walking toward the fence where Sky was tied up and Marie Lee was chasing a butterfly. And when I saw his shoulders slump, something inside of me ignited with anger. He was such a beautiful, strong, capable man. He deserved to walk with his head held high, and his gut full of pride. I didn't know who the hell he was talking to, but I already wanted to strangle them for ruining his morning.

I watched him disappear back around the guesthouse before Marie Lee squealed. And without another thought, I abandoned my coffee and went back out to the window by the front door.

"All right, princess! Let's go put Sky back in her pen. Then who's ready for lunch?" Bryce asked.

"Me! Me! Me!" she exclaimed as her father scooped her up.

I heard the tension in his voice. I listened to the mock happiness he plastered on just for his daughter. I watched them as they made their way back to Sky's pen, removed her bridle and started back toward the house. And every single part of me wanted to run out and comfort him. Run out and help him. But, I resisted the urge. I needed to keep that part of me that had already fallen for Bryce in check. I couldn't let it rage out of control, not when his life was already so out of control in the first place. I drew in a deep breath as I forced myself away from the window. I let the curtain fall closed before I backtracked to get my mug of coffee. And as I stepped out onto the back patio of the guesthouse, I looked over to the corner where Bryce had been standing.

Who were you talking to?

As I sat down in one of the lounger chairs, I turned around the words I heard him spit out. On the one hand, I felt bad for eavesdropping on what seemed like a very personal conversation. But, on the other hand, I knew who he was talking about. It was something to do with his ex-wife, that much I knew for certain. I mean, why else would he need a lawyer? Why else would he sound so upset?

Then, if he was walking away so defeated...

"Oh, no," I whispered.

The man was still in love with his ex.

The more I focused on that realization; the more tears tried to prickle the backs of my eyes. I steadied my quivering lower lip by sipping my coffee, but then I just started chugging. I chugged, and I chugged until the mug was gone, then I got up and poured myself another cup just for something to do. I felt stupid for being this upset. I mean, the man was going through a divorce. What the hell had I expected!?

You've done it again, Willow.

I flopped back down into the lounger and didn't bother

fighting back the tears any longer. With my day off, I could take some time to shake my crush and apply for some other jobs. I knew I couldn't stay here, though, not after what Bryce and I had shared together. It would make things awkward, especially if he was still in love with the woman who left him. Even the thought of leaving here made me sick, but I'd make sure a wonderful nanny was appointed in my place. One that would adhere to the schedule I had already set up for her so Marie Lee wouldn't skip a beat in her development.

At least I have the whole day to apply for jobs.

After my second cup of coffee, I made my way back inside. With my robe wrapped tightly around my sore, naked body, I poured myself one last cup before I sat down at my laptop. I eased it open and started doing some research into online job applications. The first thing I did was update my resume as it had been quite a while. And after it was updated, I started submitting it along with tailored cover letters to a variety of jobs that were open around town.

Part-time work as a waitress.

Full-time work as a manager of a grocery store.

Part-time work that could turn into full-time work as a pre-k daycare.

I threw my application at anyone that would take it, really.

However, I hadn't noticed how much time I spent researching jobs. Putting in applications. Signing up for services to get my hands on more jobs to apply for. Because when a knock came at my door, and I looked up, the sun was no longer streaming through the window. The birds were no longer chirping in the morning. And it had gotten very, very dark in the guesthouse.

"What time is it?" I murmured to myself.

"Willow?" Bryce asked.

Another knock came at the door, and I froze.

"Yeah?" I called out.

"I just wanted to let you know that dinner's ready if you don't feel like cooking."

I looked down at my robe. "Give me a few minutes, and I'll be over there."

I sent off my last resume for the day and closed my laptop. Then, I quickly threw some clothes on. I tossed my hair up into a messy bun and slipped into some flip flops, then walked my ass over to have dinner with them. If I didn't come to dinner, it would seem odd. And I didn't want Marie Lee to be disappointed. But, as I sat down with them in front of my massive plate of food, I felt his eyes on me.

The entire time I was eating.

"Willow?" he finally asked.

I didn't look up at him. "Yes?"

"Would it be okay if we talked about things tonight after dinner?"

My eyes finally met him. "I'm not sure that's a good idea, Bryce."

His eyes searched mine. "Why not?"

I snickered. "Well, I technically wanted to talk with you

about something last night. However, we seem to be setting another kind of track record that might not be healthy?"

I nodded toward Marie Lee to try and signal to him that we didn't need to have this conversation in front of her. But, he seemed oblivious to my hint.

"We can stand outside and talk, then, if that works better for you."

I shook my head. "I'm just going to head to bed after dinner."

Marie Lee pouted. "No bedtime?"

Bryce took her hand. "She's got the day off, princess. Remember?"

Marie Lee looked over at me. "But... but bedtime?"

I giggled. "Sure. I can put you to bed tonight. That's not a problem."

She threw hands in the air. "Bedtime!"

Bryce sighed. "You really don't have--."

I held up my hand. "It's fine. I promise."

After dinner came the bedtime routine, and after the bedtime routine came Bryce trying to talk some sense into me. He kept trying to convince me to speak with him. To let him talk. To let him explain some things. But I didn't want to hear it. I knew the second I let that man speak up for himself, I'd fall right back into his arms. Right back into his lap. Because when it came to unavailable men, apparently I couldn't help myself.

But I had to.

For once in my life, I had to help myself.

So, with Bryce calling after me from the patio door, I made my way across the backyard. Past the pool. Around the hot tub. All the way into the guesthouse.

And when I closed the door behind me, I finally let the tears fall as I sank to my ass on the floor.

Shit.

18

Bryce

I let out a long breath as my brother continued to rattle on.

"And here's the thing about the percentages we were given. They're all based on past things our parents did. Yeah, that's right. They're drawing these predictions from things that happened twenty, thirty years ago. Back when Mom and Dad were doing shit the hard way. We've expedited this process. We've come a long way in the few years since we took on this company. And our numbers have skyrocketed. I think if we're going to get any sort of accurate prediction, we only need to be drawing from the years we've been running this company because that's when we started implementing our way of doing things."

I nodded. "Right. So, do you have those projections, taking all of this into account?"

Will grinned. "You know I do, brother."

I held out my hand, and he slapped the other file against my palm. And when I flipped open the cover, my eyes bulged.

"You're kidding," I said.

Will shook his head. "Not a damn bit. See how different the chart looks?"

"And this is just with the things we've implemented."

"Over the past seven years, yes."

My eyes scanned the graphs. "This is insane. The investors are going to love this."

"I do think we should still be transparent and show them both files."

"Oh, yeah. Definitely."

"But, I think if you take this stuff to Houston with you on that trip coming up and get it distributed while you're there, it'll save Bart a hell of a lot of footwork come the end of the year."

I snapped my folder closed. "Get it all for me in one organized folder, and I'll put it with my stuff."

My brother smiled from ear to ear. "Already done, man."

He handed me a laminated binder with charts and graphs that were color-coated, sorted by year, and then divided by my parent's reign over this company and ours. Will had the stats split as well as calculated together, and I was impressed with the level of organization this took. Will usually threw shit together at the last minute. He was always doing that kind of thing to me. But with Bart's encouragement, he had gone above and beyond.

He was on another level.

"All right. I got one more question," I said.

Will leaned back. "Hit me with it."

I peeked up from the binder. "Who are you, and what have you done to my brother?"

He barked with laughter. "Like I've said: my passion is with numbers and graphs. I know we aren't in a position to switch out the CTO we've got now. But when we do?"

I grinned. "You'll be the first considered for the job. Besides, I'm pretty sure Uncle Ryan's going to be retiring within the next couple of years. So, you won't have to wait much longer."

"Perfection in a bottle."

I turned my chair around. "Now, if you'll excuse me."

"Uh, uh, uh. Not so fast, brother."

Damn it. "What is it now?"

He scooted his chair beside mine. "How about we talk about the attitude you came in with before I hit you with all of these lovely numbers."

I turned on my computer. "I didn't come in with an attitude."

"Oh, yes, you did. Everyone felt it for miles. What gives? What's happened?"

I typed in my password. "Seriously. Nothing's happened."

"Not even with a certain ex-wife?"

I ground my teeth together. "What have you heard?"

"Dude, I haven't heard shit. But I know you. When you get this riled up? It's only because of one person. And she's the only person I've ever seen that pisses you off this much."

I sighed. "I had a conversation with Patricia's lawyer last night."

"Why the hell are you talking to Patricia's lawyer? Didn't you get your own?"

"Yeah. I did. Which is why I took the call. I wanted to know why the hell she was reaching out directly to me. Figured something was wrong since Patricia hasn't once called Marie Lee or anything."

"Fuck, man. What happened?"

I slowly turned in my chair to face him. "On top of everything Patricia has already done, and the money she's siphoned off me, and the half of my retirement and investments that she can't wait to get her grimy little hands on, she also wants fifteen percent of the family's petroleum business."

Will stared at me for a long time before he cocked his head.

"Is she huffing glue or something?"

I snickered. "I got no fucking clue. But, I told her lawyer that the only communication she'd be having with me is with my own lawyer."

"Have you actually called your lawyer, though?"

I nodded. "Late last night, when I finally settled down for bed. I told him everything that was going on, and he told me he'd reach out to Patricia's lawyer and tell them exactly what

I'll be handing over. And if they don't like it, we can go to court."

He clapped my shoulder. "I'm proud of you for finally standing up."

I shook my head. "It's never been about standing up. It's been about trying to get through this without ruining one another in the process. I don't want this to be messy. Marie Lee's been through enough. But if that woman thinks for one second, I'm handing over half of my life because she put up with me for two years after we got accidentally pregnant? She's got another thing coming."

"Can I point something out, though? Something you could probably use in court?"

"What?"

Will sighed. "She still has yet to ask for custody."

The idea made me so sick I almost reached down for the trash can beside my desk. But, my phone ringing in my pocket pulled my mind elsewhere.

"I gotta take this," I murmured.

Will hugged my neck. "We're gonna get you through this, brother. All right?"

I nodded. "Thanks."

And as Will left my office, leaving the binder behind, I picked up the call from my private investigator. I wasn't sure how much more shitty news I could take, though.

"Detective," I said.

"Mr. Remington. I wanted to call and inform you that I'm

pretty sure your ex-wife is now working under the assumption that she's being tailed."

I leaned back. "Sounds like a personal problem."

"Have you told anyone that is in contact with her about the fact that you've hired me?"

I shrugged. "Just my brother. But, no one else knows. Oh, my lawyer now knows. But that's it."

"And you're sure your brother isn't in contact with her or anything?"

I chuckled. "He'd rather set himself on fire."

"All right. Well, then you've got a very perceptive ex-wife."

I furrowed my brow. "Why do you think she knows you're following her?"

"Her movements have changed drastically. She isn't going to the usual places she's frequented over the past few weeks. She isn't meeting up with friends any longer. And I still can't find her with any sort of a guy on her arm. I'm no closer to figuring out who in the world she's left you for, but this drastic change in her patterns either suggests that she knows she's being watched, or that she's under threat."

I paused. "Under threat?"

"I've seen it a few times before. If someone feels as if they are under threat for some reason, they're patterns change. They go to different places to try and throw off whoever they feel might be tracking them down."

"That doesn't sound like Patricia."

He paused. "Well, where do you want to go from here?"

I pinched the bridge of my nose. "Can we shift gears for a second?"

"You keep paying the invoices, and I'll do whatever you need."

I chuckled bitterly. "Thanks. Uh, I've got some issues cropping up with the divorce. This woman you're tailing, my ex? She's demanding a great deal of my financial assets. Still, she has asked about nothing in the way of custody regarding our daughter."

"That's a bit odd."

"Yes, it is. I'd like you to start digging into her life to see if you can find anything at all I can use in court. Because I know once she figures out that I denied her hefty financial requests, she'll come at me with all she's got."

"I can definitely do that. Heading to my office now. I can start with phone and bank records, and work my way out from there."

"I appreciate it, thanks."

"No problem, Mr. Remington. I'll be in touch."

As I hung up the phone, I felt like I was sinking. I felt like I was bobbing in the middle of the ocean with no life raft, no paddle, and nothing to eat or drink. First, my ex-wife leaves. Then, the divorce. And then, Willow came charging head-first into my life like a bull out of its pen, and now I've fucked even that up!

"God damn it!" I roared.

I slammed my fists against my desk and felt the wood beneath it crack. I stood up from my chair, pacing around my office as anger grew within me. I couldn't remember the last time I'd been this sick with rage. My ex-wife wanted to financially rake me over the coals after she left me for someone else? My perfect nanny wants nothing to do with me after I couldn't keep my hands to myself?

And the only one paying for any of this was my fucking daughter.

Maybe I shouldn't have custody, either.

I raked my hands down my face. I had to get away from everything for a while. Then, it hit me. When the hell exactly was that business trip to Houston?

I scrambled back to my chair and pulled up my schedule before a smile crossed my face.

"Perfect," I murmured.

I typed away at my desk, contacting the hotel I was booked with. The weekend conference started Friday, but if God wanted to smile upon me, I'd be able to back up my reservation a few days. Hell, I could make it a week-long thing, get the hell out of here for a while, and clear my head before coming back home.

And after backing up my reservation three whole days, I stood to my feet.

"Time to get going," I said to myself.

After rearranging my schedule and shooting an email off to Will and Bart about the change in plans, I closed up my office for the day. My check-in time was before midnight this evening. So, I decided to take the convertible I kept cooped up in the garage and drive it to Houston. I would enjoy the nice road trip with the top down and a milkshake in the front seat beside me. Then, I would spend five days in Houston, where I got to enjoy their outstanding barbecue and sweet tea before the three-day conference started on Friday.

I raced home and headed straight for my bedroom because I couldn't wait to get the hell out of this city any longer even though the girls were outside playing. And I didn't want anything distracting me in the process.

19

Willow

I could've sworn I heard Bryce pull up in the driveway while we were out back. But, I didn't see him come outside of the garage. So, now that Marie Lee was at the dinner table for her snack time, I made my way up the stairs.

"Bryce?" I called out.

"In my room," he called back.

I walked up the rest of the stairs and made my way down the hallway. His bedroom door was cracked, and I heard his soft footsteps padding aimlessly around his bedroom. My heart seized in my chest as I ran down all the things that could possibly be wrong. But, when I eased his door open and leaned against the doorway, I didn't expect to see a gigantic suitcase against his mattress.

"Going somewhere?" I asked.

He turned away from his closet. "Yep. Got a conference in Houston."

"Oh! That seems a bit... last minute."

"Well, the conference is this weekend, but I've got other business in Houston as well. So, I figured I'd go a few days early and knock out two birds with one stone."

I crossed my arms over my chest. "So, you'll need me to hold down the fort while you're gone?"

He peeked over at me. "If you could, I'd really appreciate it. I've already transferred extra money into your account in case you want to order pizza one night, and generally for the overtime it'll take for you to be here with my daughter while I'm gone."

I nodded slowly. "I appreciate that, thanks."

"Not a problem."

When should I tell him?

"Oh! One more thing," he said.

My eyebrows rose. "I'm all ears."

He pointed at me. "I'd like you to sleep in the main house while I'm not here. It'll make me feel better to know an adult is actually in the house with her."

"Oh, of course. I'll put myself up in the guest bedroom down the hall."

"I really appreciate it."

Now. Tell him now. "So, I've got some--."

He held up his finger. "Sorry! Sorry. One more thing. Marie Lee has a doctor's appointment I scheduled for her on Thursday. I'll leave her pediatrician information behind. I noticed she had a little rash on the backs of her legs, and I wanted to get a doctor's opinion on it."

"Noted. So, I wanted to talk with you about--."

Marie Lee's voice drifted up the stairs. "All done!"

I sighed. "Right."

Bryce grinned. "Duty calls."

"But, we do need to talk before you leave. Okay? I've got news."

He nodded. "Sure, whatever you want. Just let me finish packing, and we can talk."

That never happened, though.

As I was wiping Marie Lee down in the bathroom, Bryce got a phone call that took him out to the front porch. After sitting Marie Lee down with the activity she chose in her little living room corner, I made my way back upstairs and found Bryce's stuff only half-packed. He had clothes laid out on his bed, but not all of them had been packed away.

So, I took the liberty of packing everything up and setting it off to the side.

He needs to know. Even if you have to leave a note.

I curled my nose up at the voice in my head. Leave him a note? Hell, no. This needed to be a face to face conversation. But, as I made my way out of Bryce's bedroom, something hanging on the door caught my eye.

And when I saw it was a suit, my jaw hit the floor.

"Bryce is a suit guy?" I breathed.

I reached out, running my fingertips over the soft material. It didn't take a genius to know that this suit was incredibly expensive, but it felt so wonderful against my skin. I spread my hand against the breast pocket, imagining what he might look like in a suit.

And when my thighs started warming, I quickly scampered out of his bedroom.

I needed to be watching his daughter, anyway.

"Such a weak little idiot," I hissed to myself.

When I came around the corner of the living room, though, I didn't find Marie Lee playing. Or coloring. Or reading a book. Instead, I found her sprawled out on her fluffy rug, snoring softly to herself. I cupped my hand over my mouth to stifle my giggling. The poor girl was so exhausted that she had fallen asleep without her blanket or anything! So, I scooped her into my arms and walked her upstairs, settling her down in her own bed.

But, when I pulled away, something happened.

It was something I never expected.

"No, no, no. No leave," she murmured.

Her hands tightened against my clothes as she pulled me into bed with her.

"Stay," she yawned.

I heard the front door open. "Hey, I think Daddy's back home."

Marie Lee started softly snoring again, though, which meant I could try and sneak away. When I heard Bryce's footsteps coming up the stairs, I figured I could exchange myself with him. I mean, a girl wanted to fall asleep with her Daddy anyway, right?

But, just as Bryce got to the door, I tried to move. And Marie Lee's grip on me only tightened further.

"No, no, Wiwwow. Stay."

I kissed her forehead. "But, Daddy's here."

"No, Daddy. Only you."

Her words gave me pause. So much pause, in fact that I stopped breathing. When my lungs finally drew in the much-needed air, though, I looked over toward the door.

I found Bryce staring at me with a look I couldn't interpret.

I cleared my throat. "I, uh... took the liberty of packing the rest of your suitcase. I packed up the clothes you had piled up on your bed."

He nodded slowly but didn't say anything. His eyes just kept staring at me. And the more he stared, the more vulnerable I felt.

"I'll just stay here for a bit," I whispered.

I wasn't sure how long I laid there, but eventually, Marie Lee turned away from me. And when she let me go, I eased myself out of the bedroom. I needed a drink. A stiff drink, a nap, and a fucking reality check.

"Seems like you've become part of the family," Bryce said.

Not the reality check I needed. "Can we talk for a second, if you have time?"

I turned around and watched Bryce's smile falter, and it filled me with guilt.

"That depends," he said.

I closed his daughter's bedroom door. "On what?"

"Do we need wine, sparkling cider, or standing on the porch?"

I blushed at his words. "Uh, maybe standing on the porch with some distance between us?"

He pouted playfully. "Doesn't sound like much fun."

"Well, it's not going to be a fu--."

His cell phone started ringing in his pocket, and he raised his finger, stopping me in my tracks. Of course, the one moment I had him alone to talk about this like an adult, something *else* interrupted us. I was ready to tug that man downstairs, push him into a chair, and blurt out the news he needed to know sooner rather than later.

But, as I watched him answer his phone, I knew it wouldn't happen today.

"Ten minutes," he mouthed.

I nodded, but I knew damn good, and well, we'd never get back to it.

Still, I headed downstairs anyway. I grabbed a couple bottles of water and headed out to the patio, waiting anxiously for him to show up. But, when ten minutes passed, I cracked open one of the water bottles and chugged it back.

I'll give him ten more minutes.

And after ten more minutes passed, I cracked open the other bottle and chugged.

Five more, then I'll get on my way.

After waiting forty minutes like an idiot, I heard his car zooming down the driveway, and I abandoned my post. I walked across the backyard and made my way for the guesthouse, where my eyes gravitated toward my laptop. I walked over slowly and sat down, staring at the email I left up on my screen.

It was an email with an attached acceptance letter that had been emailed to me.

It was regarding my new job.

"Shit," I hissed.

I closed the laptop and crossed my legs at my ankles. I chewed on the bed of my fingernails, racking my brain for what to do. I couldn't just dump this information on him. But, I had to let him know that I was starting a new job in a couple of weeks. That meant I only had two weeks to get my ass moved out, get a new nanny hired that I approved of, and get Marie Lee transitioned into the care of this new nanny. And now, he'd be gone for five of those days? Before we could even talk?

"Not good. This is not good."

I looked down at my cell phone and reached for it. I knew the girls would have advice for me. And since I hadn't spoken with them in a while, they were well overdue for an update anyway. With the baby monitor hooked to my hip and cranked up all the way, I dialed Sadie's number. And before she even picked up, I called Luna. Connecting her to the phone call so the three of us could talk.

"Girl! It's been forever. I don't like this. You need more days off," Sadie said.

"I'm sure you've got some juicy details for us, though, right?" Luna asked.

"I mean, the town is ablaze with chatter about Patricia and Bryce."

"Did you hear about her demands? She wants fifteen percent of that man's company!"

"I heard she wants all of his investment accounts, too."

"And his retirement."

I blinked. "Uh, sorry. What?"

Sadie paused. "You don't know?"

Luna snickered. "How the hell could you not know? You live with the man."

I furrowed my brow. "What *exactly* have you guys heard?"

As they started talking over one another, filling me in on the insanity of Bryce's divorce, my stomach dropped to the floor. No wonder he had been so defeated after that conversation I overheard. No wonder his shoulders had been slumped. He wasn't defeated because he still loved her. He felt defeated because of the demands she was making with money she thought she was entitled to.

But, solving that mystery posed yet another question.

What the hell had Bryce wanted to talk about today on the porch?

20

Willow

"Sparkies!" Marie Lee exclaimed.

Thunder rolled like a truck down the highway as lightning cracked across the sky.

"That's right, pretty girl. That's called 'lightning.'"

"Nu-uh."

"Mhm."

"Nu-uh!"

I giggled. "Then, what's it called, smartypants?"

She beamed with pride. "Daddy calls them 'sparklies.' And Daddy's always right."

I had to curl my lips over my teeth to keep from barking with laughter. The image of Bryce in his big ole' Dad voice saying something like 'sparklies' made me want to laugh and cry at the same time. I'd miss these two a lot. Especially since I wouldn't get to say goodbye formally because of this business trip, Bryce left for yesterday.

"More sparklies!" she exclaimed.

We sat perched at the window, watching the summer storm roll on in. The rain kicked up dust that I knew would settle on the trucks. So, I had plans for Marie Lee and me to wash them tomorrow. A fun activity with colorful bubbles and water hoses. I mean, I wasn't sure about her, but that sounded like my two-year-old fantasy in a nutshell. I was looking forward to it, as well. Any time I got with her between now and the end of the week was just fine with me. And now that we were alone with no one to interrupt us, I could devote all of my time and energy to her.

Like I should have been doing from the beginning.

"All right, pretty girl. It's snack time. What would you like?" I asked.

Marie Lee clung to me as I picked her up. "Jewwo?"

I snickered. "You know you only get one sweet treat a day. Do you want it to be Jello at snack time?"

I watched her think really hard about it as her brow furrowed and her lips pursed together. She looked as if she were in deep thought, so I got her set up at the table while she pondered her choices in her mind. I meandered into the kitchen and found myself taking in every little detail—the shining granite countertops with flakes of silver twinkling inside. The beautiful white-washed cabinets with matte black handles that somehow made the room seem more modern than laid-back country. I peeked down at the rich hardwood floors that looked original with the house itself, shimmering with a fresh wax and not a scuff to be seen.

"Wiwwow?"

I looked over at the sweet girl. "Made a decision?"

But, before she could answer, a heavy knock came at the door.

I furrowed my brow just like Marie Lee's as I silently told her to stay put with my hand. I wandered over to the door and tried to see through the frosted window, but all I saw was a blurry outline of someone. Even through the blurriness, though, the features seemed familiar—someone short, with what looked like blonde hair and--.

"Patricia?" I whispered.

I quickly opened the door, and she turned around, looking like a sopping wet dog in the middle of a July downpour. And the angry look in her eye as her gaze fell down my body told me everything I needed to know about the tone of her visit.

"You're Bryce's new flavor of the month, I take it?" she spat.

I blinked. "No, ma'am. I'm the nanny. Can I help you?"

She pushed past me. "I'm here for my daughter."

And before I even thought about what I was doing, I reached out and grabbed her wrist. Preventing her from moving anywhere.

"I'm sorry, you're what?" I asked as I kicked the door closed.

"Get off me," she warned.

"I think Bryce would be just fine with this current altercation. Why are you here to get Marie Lee?"

Her eyes narrowed. "Because she's my daughter."

"One that you abandoned almost two months ago."

She wrenched away from my grasp. "How dare you accuse me of such a thing. I don't even know you!"

"I know plenty about you, though."

She harrumphed. "I don't give a damn what you've heard about me. I'm here to get my daughter now that I'm all set up in a new place, and that is that. Marie Lee!?"

"Mom?"

"I'm calling Bryce. And if he tells me that you're not supposed to be--."

She ignored me and walked off toward the kitchen, screaming for her daughter. So, I rushed up to her and grabbed her arm, tugging her away from the table. And as I tried fishing around in my pocket for my cell phone while trying to fight this woman, I realized I didn't have it on me. I ran after Patricia as she stormed up to the table, unbuckling Marie Lee and scooping her into her arms.

And the way Marie Lee fought her made me sick.

"No, Mom!"

Patricia held her close. "Come on, honey. I've got a place all nice and set up for us."

"No! I don't wanna! Wiwwow!"

I gripped her arm again, trying to level her with a glare. But, all she did was buck up to me, and I didn't know what else to do.

"I'm calling the police if you don't let me go, you sorry sack of nonsense," Patricia threatened.

"Give me your cell phone. I'm calling Bryce right now to ask him about this," I said.

She shrugged. "I don't have to do anything for you, *nanny*."

"I've been more to this girl in the past few weeks than you've been in that same amount of time. And I think if we put that in front of any police officer, they'll agree with me. Now, we either call Bryce--."

She wrenched away again. "Let me guess. He fucked you, right?"

I blinked. "You shouldn't use that kind of language in front of Marie Lee. Even at this young of an age."

She giggled bitterly. "He screwed around with you, gave you a glass of wine, cuddled up with you on that couch, and somehow you just couldn't resist him. Right?"

I swallowed hard. "Give me your phone."

She took a step toward me. "I'm not giving you anything, and here's why: I'm that little girl's mother, and you're just Bryce's new play toy. That man never cared for me. The only reason why he married me was because of the daughter we had. There's no sin in finding me a man that cares for both my daughter and me. I matter, too. So, we'll put that in front of a judge and see what they have to say. But, in the meantime? I'm taking my daughter even if I have to fight off the lowly nanny my ex-husband is screwing around with in his spare time."

But still, I only tightened my grip. Refusing to let go as

Marie Lee looked up at me in horror. Still, this woman was stronger than she looked, and she pulled away from me as if I had butter on my hands. And when I reached out for her once more, she dodged me before she whipped around and leveled a stare at me that made my heart stop in my chest.

"You put your hands on my daughter or me again, and I'll have you arrested. Understood?"

Marie Lee started crying. "No!"

I looked at the precious little girl. "I'll figure something out, pretty girl. Don't you worry, okay?"

I watched in horror as that woman carried the screaming and kicking girl over her shoulder and toward the front door. Everything within me wanted to pummel that woman to the ground before tossing her out into the cold rain. But, I resisted the urge.

"Wiwwow! Pwease! No!"

Tears rushed my eyes as the little girl reached out for me.

"Daddy!" she shrieked.

I heard Patricia hiss. "Calm down, now. You're just fine. You're with Mommy."

"No, want Mommy!"

As the front door opened and slammed shut, a tear trickled down my cheek. There was so much to unpack about what just happened. It was unreal. But, the interaction only solidified what I needed to do. First, I needed to call Bryce. After that, though, I needed to leave him a note and start packing up my things.

I was more than just a nanny.

I was more than a fuck toy.

And Marie Lee deserved a nanny that would focus more on her and less on her father.

I dashed back out to the guesthouse, and the first thing I did was rush for my cell phone, still on the charger, untouched from this morning. I found Bryce's number in my contacts and pressed 'call' even though I knew he'd be busy, and of course, it went straight to his voicemail. I pinched the bridge of my nose as his voice filled my ear. I sat down gingerly, still hearing the echoed yellings of his daughter bouncing off the walls of my mind.

Then, it came time for me to leave a voice message.

"Bryce, hey. It's me. Listen, I know you're busy. But I just, I'm so... so sorry..."

My mind fell blank, and I hated myself for it.

"Look, Patricia's come by and took Marie Lee. I tried to stop her.. But...but she *is* Marie Lee's mother. Just... your daughter needs you right now, okay? She didn't want to go with her mother."

I need you right now.

"Yeah, so. All right. Let me know what to do. I'm so sorry, Bryce. I couldn't stop her."

I hung up the phone and slid it into my pocket as I walked like a zombie into the kitchen. I heard an engine revving down the road, and it made me sick to think about Marie Lee sitting in the back seat of some speeding car trying to whisk her away from the only home she'd ever known. I wiped at my tears as they streamed down my neck. My chest soon started heaving with my sobs. And as I flopped into a seat at the kitchen table, I pulled my laptop towards me.

But, leaving a voice message or sending an email seemed so impersonal.

Maybe leaving a handwritten note would be better.

I lumbered back over into the house, and the first person I encountered was Maria. Some weeks, it felt like I didn't see her at all. She was always careful not to interrupt. But, the expression on her face caused me to pause. There was a mixture of worry and sadness: fury and sorrow. But, there was something else in her eye that I couldn't interpret.

Something I was too tired to interpret.

"Pen and paper?" I asked softly.

Maria simply pointed to a cabinet towards the corner of the kitchen.

"Thanks," I whispered.

With a heavy heart and even heavier shoulders, I blinked back tears as I rummaged around for a pen. And after pulling out a notepad to scrawl on, I started writing Bryce the note. I hated that we couldn't have this talk in person. But, maybe this was all for the best. Me never seeing him again. Me calling the police so they can figure out what the hell to do about Marie Lee. Me getting the hell out of this place before I lost my mind, my heart, and my dignity all over again.

"He's gonna miss you, you know," Maria said.

Her thick accent turned my head, and I found her wiping down the kitchen table where Marie Lee had just been sitting.

"A lot," she then added.

But instead of fighting back, I simply let my eyes fall back to my note. I kept my hand as steady as I could, murmuring the words to myself. Making sure the note flowed effortlessly and didn't seem as disjointed as my mind currently felt.

Then, I picked it up and read it one last time to myself once the tears dried up.

Dearest Bryce,

I've taken a full-time office position with a warehouse on the other side of town. I start at the end of the month. Thank you for all the generosity you showed me, and I wish you to best of luck with your divorce.

W.

I took the note and taped it to the fridge so it wouldn't flutter anywhere. And then? I started back out to the guesthouse. I needed to get packing and get back to my place if I stood any chance at starting this job in a week and a half. I kept trying to convince myself that Marie Lee was safe with Patricia because she was her mother, and this upcoming job would be good for me. That nothing terrible would come of any of this, and everyone would get the lives they always dreamt about.

But even as I started packing up my things, I knew that wasn't the case. I knew I was running. I knew I was doing that thing I always did again.

And yet, I was still helpless to stop myself as I started stacking my toiletries into my cosmetics bag.

21

Bryce

It felt good to be in Houston. It felt good to be out of that gossiping small town and away from the craziness my life had become. And while some of it was a good kind of crazy, a great deal of it was still the bad kind. The kind I wanted to get away from. The kind I never wanted to encounter again.

The kind that was about to take half of everything, plus part of my family's business.

"Shit," I whispered.

As I settled into my hotel suite, I eased myself against the mattress. Still clad in one of the only four suits I owned, I gazed up at the ceiling. I was glad I came early so I could enjoy a couple of days to myself. But, the day after tomorrow marked the start of a long weekend of work. One where I'd have to buckle down, get shit done, and get some things finalized.

However, my cell phone vibrating in my pocket ripped me from my trance.

"What is it now?" I sighed to myself.

I looked at the phone and saw the house number was calling. So, it had to be Marie. Willow would've just called me on my cell phone since she had my number. I answered the phone and drew in a deep breath, steeling myself against whatever it was that was so urgent it required a phone call while I was out of town.

"Hello, Maria," I said.

"Mr. Remington. I hope I'm not bothering you?"

Her accent always made me smile. "Not at all. Everything okay?"

"Well, sir. No. That's why I'm calling."

I rubbed the back of my neck. "What's going on? Is Marie Lee alright?"

The second she launched into her spiel, her accent took over. Some of the words she started slinging around were even in Spanish. I heard the worry in her voice. The anger. The confusion. But, I knew enough of the language simply by being around her to understand what she was telling me.

"Hold, hold, hold, hold, hold on just a second. Did you say Patricia came to get Marie Lee?" I asked.

"*Sí*."

"And Willow just... let her have my daughter?"

"I don't think she understood what was supposed to do. She did fight, Mr. Remington. But, your ex-wife threatened her with police and all sorts of stuff. She was crying, sir. Your daughter didn't want to go. I don't know what to do."

"Where's Willow? Where is she?"

She paused. "She wrote you a note before she headed back out to the guesthouse, and she hasn't come back."

I quickly sat up, and noticed I had a voicemail from Willow. "A note? Those are never good in my world. Can you read it for me?"

"Isn't that an invasion of privacy, Mr. Remington?"

I tried not to groan. "All right. Look. I'm going to check out early and head back. But, until then? No one else is allowed on the property. Not until I get back and get things sorted out. Understood? Call the sheriff if she comes back. I'll call him to explain as soon as we are done talking."

"*Si.*"

I stood to my feet. "Good."

"Sir, may I speak freely?"

I paused. "I didn't realize you thought you had to ask."

She giggled. "Sir, I know it's not my place. But, Willow is the first person to come into your home that truly makes you smile. No disrespect to the mother of your child, but I've never seen you look at her the way you look at Willow. It's nice to see you smiling again, sir."

I grinned at her comment. "It's *our* house, Maria. You're just as much of a part of this family, and you know that."

"That's very kind, Mr. Remington. Thank you."

I walked over to my suitcase. "I'm packing up now. I'll call you once I'm on the highway. And when I get home? We're going to figure out what to do next. That woman isn't keeping my daughter. She doesn't get to leave me for someone else, demand all of my money, and then take our daughter after radio silence for weeks now. That isn't happening."

"No, sir."

"I'm glad we're on the same page. I'll call you soon."

"I'll be here, sir."

I started throwing my things back into my suitcase. "On second thought, Maria? Take the weekend off. Hell, take the entire week off. Paid leave."

She paused. "*Lo Siento?*"

"Take the week off, Maria. Go spend it with your husband. Go visit the grandkids. Go do something for yourself. It's paid time off. I won't count it against your vacation."

She sighed. "Oh, *gracias*, Mr. Remington."

"Bryce, damn it. You're part of this family. 'Bryce' is just fine."

I heard the smile in her voice. "Thank you, Bryce. Really."

"Now, go on. Enjoy the week. And when you get back, I promise everything will be all right."

"Bryce!"

I paused. "Yes?"

"There's... something else."

I blinked. "I'm all ears, Maria."

She sighed. "Don't be mad at me."

I braced myself. "I'd never be upset with you for simply confiding in me. What is it? What's wrong?"

The silence from her was deafening. "So, my sister. She lives and works in Houston, right?"

"Actually, I didn't know that. Had I known, I would've paid her a visit and said 'hello' from you."

"I didn't know you were in Houston, exactly. Just that you were on a business trip."

I waved my hand in the air. "Doesn't matter. What is it you want to tell me?"

She started talking quickly again. "Well, sir—I mean, Bryce—my sister works for a veterinarian office. I never really paid attention to all that nonsense because when we get together, we talk about anything other than work. *Si*, so I figured out that she doesn't just work for any veterinarian's office. Your vet? Dr. Morris? He has a second vet office in Houston."

"The one your sister works for."

"*Si*."

"What does this have to do with me?"

She sighed heavily. "My sister sent me a picture. She thought she was sending me a nice, juicy piece of gossip about her boss that we could giggle over, but you really need to see it."

"Do you know my cell number?"

Silence hung on the other end of the line before my phone lit up against my face.

"There. I sent it," Maria said.

I moved the phone away from my ear and opened up the text. And when I saw the image, my gut almost bottomed out through my asshole.

"Maria, when did you get this picture?" I asked.

She paused. "*Lo Siento*, sir. I-I-I mean, Bryce I, uh, I got it just after you left. You know, for your trip? I figured I'd show it to you when you got back. Then, everything happened so fast, and Patricia was here and--."

"Sh, sh, sh, sh, sh. It's okay. Take a breath. I'm not upset with you."

She sighed. "Promise?"

I nodded. "I promise. I'm not upset. But, what I want you to do is keep that picture. Save it to your phone, and don't delete it until I tell you to. Okay?"

"*Si*, Bryce."

"And go home. Let me take care of everything else. Give yourself a week to just enjoy your life."

"Are you sure?"

I smiled softly. "I'm more than sure. You just gave me something they call leverage, and I have a feeling things are going to be just fine from now on."

I hung up the phone and shoved it into my pocket. It didn't take me any time at all to throw my things into the suitcase and zip it up. I didn't even double-check to make sure I wasn't leaving anything behind, either. If I left it, I could buy a new one. Simple as that. But, I had to get back home before Willow did something incredibly stupid...

...like leave.

"Mr. Remington, is everything all right?" the front desk attendant asked.

I slid her the key to my room. "Family emergency. I have to go. Thank you for your hospitality."

"Of course, sir. Is there anything you--!?"

I rushed out of the automatic front doors of the hotel lobby before the woman even finished her sentence. I had to get home. I had to make things right. I had to be the glue that held this family together before everything fell apart on me. I'd already done that once. Hell, I was still suffering from the fallout of my family, failing one time.

I wouldn't fail my family again.

"Come on," I grumbled, calling Willow for the third time after listening to her voicemail message. And for the third time listening to her voicemail greeting.

After tossing my luggage into the back of my convertible, I hopped into the front seat. I peeled out of the hotel parking lot without a second thought, almost running over the valet attendant. I ignored how hungry my stomach was as I passed by fast-food joints. Coffee shops. Diners and restaurants that were still open well past regular dinner time hours. I put the pedal to the metal as I careened onto the interstate, my tires squealing as I weaved in and out of traffic.

And with the wind in my hair, I felt my strength coming back. I felt my balls reattaching themselves. I dug down deep to find the one part of my manhood that hadn't been completely obliterated, and I tugged it--kicking and screaming--to the forefront.

No matter what it took from me, I had to put us back together. Myself, Willow, and Marie Lee had to be fixed.

And my ex-wife?

Well, she could go fuck the man she left me for and be happy with the decision she made.

I SQUEALED INTO MY DRIVEWAY JUST AFTER MIDNIGHT AND didn't bother unpacking my things. Hell, I didn't bother taking the damn keys out of the ignition! I used the spare key under the mat to unlock the door, throwing my shoulder into it just in case it decided to stick on me again. These humid summers could kiss my ass when it came to owning a log cabin-style ranch house on a bazillion acres of nothing but trees. Hot and wet as could be, and the house ballooned like my ex-wife on her period.

"Willow!" I exclaimed.

I rushed to the back of the house and stormed onto the porch, only to be greeted with a lifeless backyard.

"Willow!" I roared noting her truck wasn't parked beside the guest house.

After nothing but the echoing of my voice bounced back at me, I retreated back into the kitchen—the note. Where the hell was this note, Maria had spoke of? I finally found a piece of paper taped to the refrigerator. I walked up to it as my eyes scanned through the words, but I had to murmur it to myself in order to process it.

"Dearest, Bryce. I've taken a full-time office position with a warehouse on the other side of town. I start at the end of the month. Thank you for all the generosity you showed me, and I wish you--no, no, no, fucking hell no!"

I ripped the note off the fridge and dashed to the sink. I stuffed the fucking thing down the garbage disposal before flipping on the faucet. I jammed my hand against the switch and listened to that paper shred before it got washed down the drain.

"No," I whispered.

I turned the disposal and the water off before I leaned against the counter. With the heels of my hands pressed into my eyes, I forced my mind to settle down. I had to think this through. I couldn't let my fucking family fall apart twice because of my bitch-ass ex. She had screwed around with me for the last time, and I wasn't going to take it any longer. So, I ripped my phone out of my pocket and dialed Pat's number.

And the first sound I heard before her voice even hit my ears was Marie Lee crying in the background.

I shook with fury as her voice finally appeared. "What?"

I scoffed. "What do you mean, what? Where the hell do you get off storming into my house and kidnapping your daughter?"

She barked with laughter. "Kidnap!? She's my daughter! More mine than she ever was yours."

I narrowed my eyes. "What the hell docs that mean?"

"It means while you were out working all these hours and

training all these animals and going to all these rodeos, I was the one actually *raising* her."

"Daddy!" Marie Lee cried out.

I heard Patricia shush her, and my head almost blew through the roof.

My blood boiled. "Don't you shut our daughter up when she's calling out for me. You hear me?"

"I'm done with this phone call. Call me when you can--."

The words flew from my mouth like wildfire. "I've got court-ordered documents that state you'll get nothing if we don't meet up to talk about this."

She snickered. "You're bluffing. I know you. You've only given those divorce papers one good looking through. Enough to be pissed off at me for absolutely no reason."

"You want fifteen percent of a business that has nothing to do with you!"

"Because I had to put up with your insufferable, absent ass for two years, Bryce. Two damn years, and you didn't give me shit except for a stretch-marked body, a spoiled daughter, and no future to look forward to whatsoever."

Now, my momma taught me never to harm a woman. Never to lay even a pinky on her unless she wanted it. But, at that moment? I dreamt of all the ways I'd slaughter that woman if she ever stepped foot back into this house.

"Patricia, I'm giving you one last chance to just come over and talk. Bring Marie Lee back, and we can settle this like adults," I said calmly.

She scoffed. "Or you'll what?"

I sighed. "Well, since you've got a pretty sparkling diamond ring on your finger in this picture I have of you with Dr. Morris, I'd assume you're planning some sort of a wedding. And I'd figure you might need the money from me. You want to start your new life."

She paused for a long time. "I knew you had someone following me, you sick fuck."

I grinned. "You're right. I hired a private investigator. But, I didn't get this information from him."

"You're lying."

"That's fine if you think so. Doesn't change the truth. You were good at dodging my P.I. But, what you failed to do was get to know the people around you while you were living with me."

"What!?"

"Maria's sister works for Dr. Morris's clinic down there in Houston. That's how I got my hands on this fun little picture I've got stored on my phone. Not everyone likes him, you know."

About a minute's worth of silence passed, except for the occasional sniffle from my daughter in the background.

"Pat."

She finally spoke. "What?"

"I'll agree to your terms, in a roundabout way, in the divorce papers if you just come over so we can talk. Like adults."

"Fine. When?"

"Tomorrow. For lunch. Be here at noon, and bring Marie

Lee. You don't bring our daughter? I let this picture loose across town. We'll see how that kind of gossip holds up in court around here since our divorce is filed in the same county where we got married."

She growled. "I hate you."

"Trust me, the sentiment is mutual. Noon. Here. Otherwise, you know what I'll do."

Then, I hung up the phone and readied myself for a long, sleepless night.

22

Willow

After leaving last night to go back to my old apartment, I woke up with the sunlight beating against my face. I rolled over and pressed a pillow over my head, hoping to sleep the entire day away. I didn't want to get up. I didn't want to go anywhere. I didn't want to get involved with anything or see anyone or do the things I knew I had to do.

Like go back to Rocking R Ranch and pick up the rest of my shit.

"Ugh," I groaned.

I slid the pillow off my face and was shocked to find that it was already noon. My eyes bulged, and I leaped out of bed, heading straight for my bathroom. The stale smell of unmoving air was still pungent, but I blocked it out. After turning on all the fans in my place last night, I figured I'd leave the windows cracked after I left to go get my things. Surely, the smell would be gone by then.

Hopefully...

After cleaning myself up and putting on a loose-fitting dress, I headed back to Bryce's place. But, when I pulled up into the driveway, I saw someone storming out of the front door. The woman looked familiar, and that tight-lipped expression gave way to a reddened face I placed almost immediately.

What the hell was Patricia doing at the house again?

I pulled up behind Bryce's truck and watched with raised eyebrows as the long-legged woman slammed herself into her car. Without so much as glancing in my direction, she put the car in reverse. Only, it wasn't until I turned around and saw the windshield of her car head-on that I realized she wasn't the one driving.

Then, my jaw hit the floor.

"Doctor Morris!?" I exclaimed.

His eyes briefly held mine before he threw the car into 'drive'. Then, he and Patricia peeled off down the road. I scrambled out of my truck as my eyes widened in realization. Holy shit, was that the other woman in Dr. Morris' life.

My fling was the man Patricia left Bryce for?

"God, what a world of disappointment she's in for," I murmured to myself.

"Willow."

Bryce's voice sent warm shivers throughout my body as I turned around. And when I found him standing on the porch with his hands in his pockets, he looked as cool and as calm as I'd ever seen him. I didn't know what to think or feel, or even say at that moment. But, when I saw that cute little girl emerge beside him, gripping onto his legs, tears welled in my eyes.

"Marie Lee," I whispered.

"Wiwwow!" she exclaimed.

The little girl stumbled down the porch steps, running as quickly as she could. With her curls bouncing and her eyes full of happiness, I met her halfway and scooped Marie Lee into my arms. I cried into the crook of her neck as she wrapped those little arms tightly around my neck. She brought her legs up, locking them around me, seemingly trapping me in her embrace.

I fell to my knees on the soft front lawn grass and cried tears of joy.

Damn it, it felt good to see this little girl again.

"Pretty girl, are you okay? Are you hurt?"

I lifted my head and watched as she shook her head 'no.'

"Were you scared?" I asked softly.

She nodded slowly, and it killed me inside.

"Well, it's never gonna happen again. Not on my watch, okay?" I asked.

I didn't even hear Bryce approaching us until his shadow cloaked us from the sun.

"That means you're staying?" he asked.

I looked up at him with my watery eyes and found the kindest expression written across his face. He offered me his hand, and I kindly took it, still not wanting to give up the relief of his daughter's embrace. We walked inside, hand in hand, our fingers just barely intertwined. And when we got inside, he closed the door.

He swooped Marie Lee out of my arms.

"Wait, wait, wait. I just--a few more minutes?" I asked.

She giggled. "Swim time?"

I checked my watch. "Good girl. It is technically swim time."

Bryce kissed her cheek. "Why don't you go play? Then, once Willow and I are done talking, we'll both come swim. Okay?"

"Yay!"

I held up my finger. "Wait--I don't know if I should--."

But, the look on his face told me to stop talking. So, I did.

He put his daughter down, and I watched her barrel upstairs, no doubt trying to get to her swimsuit and floaties that were kept in her closet. I watched until she disappeared down the hallway, then a pressure at the small of my back ripped me from my trance.

"Come on. There's fresh sweet tea in the kitchen," he said.

And I didn't have to be told twice.

We filled our glasses with ice and poured them full in silence before we sat at the kitchen table. I felt like I was sitting on pins and needles as his eyes bored into my forehead. I tried not to chug the sweet tea too quickly, though, but damn it, this man made a good gallon. I wasn't sure how long we sat in silence. But, once he heaved that heavy sigh of his, I tried to form the words.

He beat me to it, though. "I'm sorry for what Pat did to you while I wasn't here. She didn't have my permission to take Marie Lee, and, of course, if I had suspected she would show up unannounced, I never would have left."

I nodded slowly. "I should've questioned it harder. I should've fought harder."

"You did nothing wrong, Willow. That woman is her mother. She's supposed to have her best interests at heart. You have no idea of knowing whether or not she was telling the truth."

I gazed into my glass. "That's the thing. Deep down, I knew she wasn't. And I let it happen anyway."

"You only had so much power. That's what Patricia does well. She strikes at that one area she knows you don't have full control over and twists the knife in deep. Don't blame yourself."

I nodded slowly. "I can do that."

"Willow."

"Yes?"

"Look at me."

I slowly lifted my eyes. "Yes?"

He grinned. "Hey there."

I blushed. "Hey there, yourself."

He chuckled. "I am sorry for what she did to you, though."

I shrugged. "It's not your fault. You couldn't have known she'd do that."

He snickered. "Shouldn't have put it past her, though. She's always been assertive and way too headstrong for her own good."

"So... care to tell me why she was here? Because I take it that it wasn't just to drop off the little one."

"No, it wasn't."

"Want to talk about it?"

He leaned back. "I mean, it wasn't much. I told her I'd give her what she wanted monetarily in exchange for full custody of Marie Lee."

My mouth fell open. "You what?"

He shrugged. "She took it without hesitation."

I blinked. "She what!?"

He snorted. "Yeah. Some mother I gave my child, huh?"

I got up and moved to the chair next to him, taking his hand. "You did everything right by that woman. You did everything you could to give her the best. She's the one who spat it back in your face, all right? Don't forget that."

His eyes fell to our connection. "You mean that?"

I squeezed his hand. "With everything I am, Bryce."

I still had questions, though. Questions I was much too curious to bury out of mere sentiment or because of 'manners.'

"Did you really give her fifteen percent of your company?" I asked softly.

He sighed heavily again. "No. I told her I would pay the

equivalent of fifteen percent of the company out to her every year until it was paid up if she dropped the alimony. I educated her on how alimony worked and how we would've had to have been married for at least four or five years before she was even eligible for it. So, she took that deal."

"What else did she take?"

His hand turned up, holding mine in return. "Half my retirement. Joke's on her, though. Only one retirement account I have is in my personal name. The rest is in the company's name with me as the beneficiary."

"I take it she doesn't have a right to those?"

"Nope," he said, popping the 'p,' "and while she'll get half of my savings account, that thing isn't as robust as she thinks it is. Our savings account is meager compared to what most people like myself have. And, she's not on the title to the house. She had terrible credit, so this house and the land and our animals? All in my name."

I whistled lowly. "I take it she didn't know that."

"Nope."

I sighed. "Wow."

He nodded slowly. "Uh-huh."

"And you think she's not going to gun for you after that?"

"She can't."

I paused. "Why not?"

He grinned. "Let's just say she's more scared of this town chewing her up and spitting her out than she is dragging my ass through the court. I'm having my lawyer draw up the edits to the divorce decree, and by the end of the day, both of us will have signed it."

I smiled. "I'm happy for you. Really."

"Thank fuck, Texas is a no-fault state."

I giggled profusely. "I've heard a couple of my friends over the years say that exact same thing."

We laughed together for a little bit before he abandoned his sweet tea to scoot closer to me. So close, in fact, that our knees touched.

My bare knees pressed against his ragged, rusted jeans.

"There's something else you should know," he said.

I paused. "What is it? What's wrong?"

"Nothing's wrong, no-no. It's just... you did come up in conversation at one point."

"Oh."

I heard Marie Lee's little footsteps as she tore into the kitchen. "I said you, not Mommy!"

I furrowed my brow. "What?"

Bryce chuckled. "That's what happened. At one point in time in our conversations, Patricia tried to get around my custody demand by asking Marie Lee, who she wanted to be with. You, or her."

Marie Lee crawled into my lap. "I said you."

I snickered. "You did now, did you?"

He let go of my hand. "She really did. And I thought Pat was going to pass out from all the blood that drained from her face."

"Maybe that'll finally show her exactly where she stands

with her daughter. Who knows? Maybe this is the wake-up call she needs to be the mother she needs to be."

"Well, she's not the only one in this equation who did wrong. She brought up a lot of good points I have to take to heart."

I cocked my head. "Like what?"

He licked his lips. "Like, spending more time here during the week and on the weekends instead of always being on the go."

I bounced Marie Lee on my knees. "That's a good point, yes."

"She accused me of being an absent father, and she was right. I threw money at our family to pay for the fact that I was working sixty hours a week, training animals, and unavailable during rodeo season because I was traveling every weekend to compete. Wasn't fair on Pat, nor was it fair on my daughter."

"You know now, and what you do with that information is what matters from here on out."

Marie Lee interjected. "Swim, pwease?"

I smiled down at her. "Just a few more minutes, okay?"

At my request, she wiggled out of my lap and rushed back upstairs. Probably to change her swimsuit to her pink one, since she had time.

The girl was going to be a handful when she got to be a teenager.

"So, that brings me to my next topic of conversation," Bryce said.

My attention turned back to him. "What's up?"

"This note you left."

"Ah."

"About the job."

I licked my lips. "Yeeeeah."

"Are you going to take it?"

I blinked. "I already have."

He nodded. "Well, un-take it."

"I'm sorry, but what?"

He took my hands within his. "Willow, in the few weeks you've been under this roof with us, you've become more like family than Marie Lee's own mother. You're the first person to make me smile like this since before I ever met Pat that night at the bar. You being here? It's good for all of us. You bring light into my life and joy into Marie Lee's. Maria adores having you around the house, and God knows you make me smile every time I see you. And I think that being here is good for you, too."

I quirked an eyebrow. "Really, now. How so?"

He grinned. "For starters, I know the job you're about to take won't pay you as well as me."

"Well, no. It won't."

"And you won't have any horses to race."

"You're right."

He scooted closer until his knee pressed against my inner thighs. "And we can talk about you having paid time off for vacation or long weekends with the girls. I bet the place you're taking that job at won't give you as much vacation time as I'm thinking."

"Mmmm, talk dirty to me, Bryce-y."

He snorted with laughter. "Does that mean you're staying? You won't leave?"

I leaned forward and kissed his lips softly, closing the distance between us.

"Yes," I whispered against his lips, "I'll stay."

He cupped the back of my head. "Give me the number, and I'll call on your behalf."

I smiled brightly. "I'm a big girl. I can make the phone call, okay?"

He gazed into my eyes. "Promise me you're staying."

My hand pressed against his heart. "I promise you, with all I am, that I'm staying."

And with a tug of his hand, our mouths crashed back together.

Sealing our deal with a sweet, luscious locking of lips.

23

Bryce
One Week Later

"Hey, princess?"

My beautiful daughter smiled from ear to ear. "Mushwooms time?"

I nodded. "Toss 'em in, beautiful."

"Yeah!"

Marie Lee took handfuls of mushrooms and started throwing them into my stir fry. She giggled with delight as I swirled the wok around, the vegetables and noodles and sauces all blending together. The steak was still in the oven, cooking to perfection in strips so we could toss as much as we wanted over our lovely mixture.

But the best part was yet to come.

Not only had Marie Lee helped me throw together a very luscious berry crumble, but we all decided to get dressed up for dinner tonight. That meant my sweet princess was in her finest princess dress with a sparkling tiara on her head, and I donned my nice, all-black suit for the occasion.

What was the best part, you ask?

Well, Willow hadn't emerged yet from the guesthouse. And I kept staring out there, wondering when I'd get to look at her outfit for the evening.

This entire week while Maria was off, felt like something out of a dream. I had my daughter back, the divorce papers had been signed, and I was officially a free man—sort of. My heart had been tethered to another woman already, and I was anxiously awaiting her arrival into the house.

The only thing she'd tell me about her ensemble was that black really suited her. So, I decided to match her with the suit I put on. After all, I wanted to make this night as memorable as possible because I had something very important to ask Willow now that she had been back with the family for a week.

I only hoped she said, 'yes.'

"Daddy?"

My daughter's voice pulled my eyes from the window. "What is it, princess?"

She pointed to the wok. "I can see the air?"

I looked down and saw my noodles were almost burning. "Shit!"

She giggled. "Diwty woody."

I coughed, waving the steam away. "Sorry, princess. You know, Daddy isn't perfect."

She clapped her hands. "Sit! Sit! Sit! Sit!"

I never thought I'd be grateful for my daughter's rising speech impediments. But, at that moment? I thanked my stars that she had one.

"All right, you little rebel. Let's get you down from the counter so Daddy can finish up," I said.

"Awwww," she pointed.

I grunted as I picked her up. "Man, you're getting big. You sure you're not ten already?"

She smiled brightly. "Someday, Daddy."

I chuckled. "Right, right."

The patio door slid open. "Mind if I join you?"

And when I looked up at the wondrous voice wafting from the glass doors, I wasn't prepared for the sight I saw.

There stood Willow, with her honey-colored eyes that matched the highlights in her chestnut hair, cloaked in a tight dress that accented her curves from head to toe. The dress shimmered with every movement she made, from the sway of her hips to the movements of her arms as she shifted her pearl-beaded black clutch in her hands. I felt my jaw swinging against the floor as she clicked toward me in her black heels. Heels that flexed her legs arched her back, and rounded out an ass my palms couldn't get enough of.

"Wow," Marie Lee whispered.

I pointed to my daughter. "My thoughts exactly."

Willow smiled. "You look nice in black, Mr. Bryce."

I grinned. "And you put me to shame, Miss Willow."

Marie Lee jumped up. "Wha' 'bout me!?"

I barked with laughter as Willow scooped my daughter into her arms. "You look like the most amazing princess I've ever laid eyes on. And that includes all the animated princesses you love so much."

My daughter beamed with pride. "You, too."

Willow smiled brightly as my daughter looked into her eyes, and I wished I would have had my camera to capture the moment. The bond those two had was some I'd never understand. But, it was also a bond I knew they'd find nowhere else. The two of them were connected on another plane. Some ethereal nonsense I never took the time to think upon or figure out. That kind of stuff was for God, not for my earthly state of mind. But, whenever I watched those two together, I was reminded of the fact that there was a higher power. There was a grander plan in all of this.

I was reminded that miracles did happen—every single day.

And I had been blessed with the best miracle of all.

"Who wants steak stir fry?" I asked.

"Me!" Willow and my daughter said together.

I smiled. "Well, let's get seated then. I'll ready our bowls and drinks and bring everything over."

Willow cocked an eyebrow. "Sure, you don't need help?"

"Nope. You just sit and enjoy."

She got my wiggling daughter into her seat at the table. "It's really all right. I can help if you need it."

"I promise, Willow. I've got it. Just sit and relax."

"You've been telling me that all week, *Bryce*."

I smiled. "Because I mean it, *Willow*."

I peered over my shoulder and saw her smiling brightly at me before she took a seat. I let my eyes sweep over her incredible outfit one last time before I started making up our bowls. I pulled glasses out of the cabinet and filled them with punch. I walked everything over to the table and made sure to serve the two most important women in my life before I served myself. And after I sat down across from my daughter and right beside Willow, I steeled myself against my nerves.

I couldn't wait a second longer to ask.

"Actually, can we pause for a second?" I asked.

Willow's fork full of food paused at her lips. "What?"

My daughter grabbed handfuls of food and shoved it into her face as my eyes locked with Willow's.

"Can I talk with you about something for a second before we eat?" I asked.

She put her fork down. "Of course. Is this a conversation for little ears, though?"

I took her hand in mind. "It's fine. I promise."

Her eyes dropped to our connection. "Bryce...?"

I drew in a deep breath. "Willow, you're part of this family. Whether you expected to be or not, that's what happened. You captured my daughter's heart and attention and respect, but you also caught mine."

She swallowed hard. "Your... what?"

I grinned. "My attention. My respect. And..."

I smoothed my thumb in soft circles as I gathered my thoughts.

"And my heart, Willow. You captured my heart in more ways than anyone on this planet ever has, and I don't want you staying in the guesthouse any longer."

Tears welled in her eyes. "You--you don't?"

I shook my head. "No. I don't. I want you in the main house like the rest of the family is. I want you to take up residence with us and get out of that stupid guesthouse. You're one of us now, and I love you. And whether you move into my room or the guest room, it doesn't matter so long as you're in the house with us."

"You--you love me?"

I brought her hand to my lips to kiss. "I do, Willow. I love you."

A tear trickled down her cheek. "You're ruining my makeup, jerk."

I reached out, wiping the tear away. "Collateral damage I'll assume responsibility for."

She sniffled before clearing her throat. "Bryce?"

"Yes?"

"I'd love to move in."

"Then, it's settled. I'll help you move all of your things--."

"And I love you, too."

I paused. "What?"

She leaned over, cupping my cheek. "I love you too, Bryce. I have for some time now."

It was time for my eyes to water. "You have no idea how happy that makes me to hear."

She smiled so brightly, her eyes closed. "Yeah, I think I have a feeling on how happy it makes you."

I wanted to kiss her so badly at that moment. I wanted to capture her lips with my own and pull her into my lap. But not in front of my daughter. Marie Lee was about to go through enough change with the divorce and Willow moving in. I wanted to try and slow things down a bit with her and what she saw. However, once we were all done with dinner, and the dishes were put away in the dishwasher, we both wasted no time in putting my daughter down for bed.

And then, we were alone.

"So, beautiful. Would you like to see your options for rooms?" I asked.

Willow grinned. "I'd love a grand tour, thank you."

I took her hand in mine. "All right. Well, across the hall from Marie Lee is one of the two guest bedrooms."

I threw open the door and flipped on the light before I held her from behind.

I settled my chin against her shoulder. "It's a basic layout. Nice queen-sized bed. Drawers with a mirror. Though this bedroom doesn't have its own bathroom. You'd be sharing with Marie Lee."

I kissed her neck softly, feeling her head fall off to the side.

"Doesn't sound too bad," she whispered.

I nibbled against her skin. "Want to see the guest bedroom downstairs? That one has a bathroom attached?"

She giggled. "Let's finish the rooms up here first."

I massaged her clothed breasts for a bit. "Sounds like a plan. Come with me."

The two of us walked hand in hand until we threw the double doors of my bedroom open. And after I took Willow's hand, I tugged her against me. Her back, seated against my stomach as her head leaned back against my shoulder.

I whispered in her ear. "This is my bedroom. It boasts of a California king-sized bed, four posters, and it's own private balcony overlooking the front yard."

She shivered. "Sounds amazing."

I nibbled on her earlobe. "The sunsets are perfect from the balcony up here."

She groaned. "Oh, I bet they are."

My hand softly slid down her stomach. "You'd have to share the ensuite with me. But, there's a double vanity."

She gasped as my fingers pressed against her clothed pussy. "My own sink."

I kissed her neck. "Mhm. And, there's a walk-in shower big enough for three as well as a jetted tub."

"Oh, Bryce."

I grinned against her bare shoulder. "You like that?"

"I love this."

"What is 'this'?"

She slowly turned around, gazing into my eyes. "This. All of it."

I slid my hand between her thighs, watching her eyes roll back. "All of this?"

Her mouth ran away from her. "All of you. All of this bedroom. All of your bathroom. Here. This is where I want to be. Now, damn it, get me in bed, you fucking tease."

I growled. "Then, why didn't you just ask?"

My hands wrapped around, gripping her luscious ass as I hoisted her against me. I kicked my doors closed before I walked her over to my bed, our lips colliding with one another. Our tongues intertwined in a familiar dance they had memorized over the last few weeks, and as our bodies fell to the mattress, I felt her body open up for me. I felt her legs spread as she welcomed me home, with my cock pressing dangerously hard against my suit pants.

"Under one condition," she breathed.

My lips hovered over her pulse point. "What?"

She cupped my cheeks, moving my eyes to meet hers. "I'll move into your bedroom under one condition."

I smiled. "Name it."

"If things get weird--or if you find this isn't what you want--just tell me. Okay?"

My eyes danced between hers. "Willow, you ain't gettin' rid of me that easily. I'm gonna hold you all night, every night, for as long as you like. And you're just gonna hafta deal with it."

She paused. "I don't think your accent's ever been that thick around me."

"Only gets thick if I got a point to prove."

She smiled softly. "Noted."

Then, my lips dropped back to hers as I cloaked her body with my own. We slithered out of our clothes, letting them fall to the floor in a bunched-up pile as my lips explored every crevice of her body. I wanted to have her like this all night. I wanted to keep her moaning and begging and shaking until she couldn't take it any longer. Until we had worked off our dinner and solidified our union a million times over.

"I love you, Bryce," she gasped.

I sank my cock between her legs as her eyes rolled back.

"I love you too, Willow. So fucking much."

Then, my headboard started thudding wildly against the wall. Creating a chorus, I wanted to hear every fucking night for the rest of my life.

I wanted to hear anything and everything to remind me that the most perfect woman on the face of this planet had somehow become mine.

EPILOGUE

Willow
Six Weeks Later

I stood at the counter in the bathroom, staring mindlessly down at the three sticks in front of me. Three of them, from the same box, and they read the exact same way. I felt my world coming to a grinding halt. I felt the rug beneath me starting to be tugged on as if this were the moment that my picture-perfect life was about to cave in on me. Up until now, everything had been working out so well for our little family of three.

Dr. Morris had closed his local office. He and Pat had moved to Houston, and we hadn't heard another word from her since the divorce papers were signed. Bryce and I had been trading off watching Marie Lee during the rodeos while we competed in our individual barrel racing events. And since I had moved in permanently, Will and Sadie were telling everyone in Conroe they were responsible for Bryce and I getting together. The joke was on them, though. They still barely spoke to each other in person, despite Luna and I encouraging Sadie to forgive Will and give him a second chance.

Now this...

What is Bryce going to say...

Suddenly nausea wafted around in my gut, threatening to bring up the little bit of breakfast I managed to get down this morning before Bryce left for work. But now, I wasn't sure if the feeling was from the shock...

... or from the fact that I was pregnant.

"Oh, no," I breathed.

My hands trembled as I picked up one of the sticks. I tilted it around, hoping that maybe a new angle of light would shed the fear away. But, no matter how I tilted the sticks and no matter what kind of light I shined against them, they were all the same.

"Holy shit, I'm pregnant," I whispered.

I shoved the sticks into the sink and washed my hands. I let the water run all over them, hoping maybe there were smudges on the screen that made these damn things look positive. I couldn't be pregnant. Not now. Not when things were going so well. I mean, I'd only moved into Bryce's room six weeks ago! It was way too soon for us to be having a child together!

We were still trying to figure out how to be a couple. And now, we had to figure out how to be parents, too?

What if I become his next Patricia?

I turned off the sink. "No. Not happening. Not by a long shot."

A knock came at the door. "What's not happening?"

Shit!

Bryce was at the door.

"Willow?" he asked, knocking again. "Everything all right?"

I tried to put on my best voice. "Yeah! Yeah, of course. Why wouldn't it be?"

"Willow..."

I snickered, trying to push the dread away. "Seriously, Bryce. I'm fine, I promise."

"Then, open the door for me."

"Why?"

"Because I'm worried about you. You've been in that bathroom for a while now."

I paused. "How long have you been home?"

He chuckled. "Willow, I didn't go to work today. Remember?"

I felt my back stiffen. My heart started beating wildly in my chest. And finally, I felt my breakfast wafting up the back of my throat. I knew I couldn't control it. I felt the room spinning as I rushed over to the toilet. I dropped to my knees and stuck my head in the bowl, trying to contain the mess I knew was about to happen.

"Willow? Open the damn door," Bryce commanded.

And the second I opened my mouth to speak, I started vomiting.

I heard banging against the door with every heave of my stomach. The door eventually burst open, though, and I heard Bryce scrambling to get to me. My hair suddenly lifted, and I felt a strong, concerned hand rubbing up and down my back. Tears streamed my face as round after round of heaving came until I was sure my stomach would turn itself inside out just to make a point.

"It's okay—I gotcha. I'm right here, beautiful," Bryce murmured.

"I'm sorry. I'm so--I'm so sor--oh, no."

A second wave hit me, and even though I had nothing to bring up, it didn't stop my stomach from rebelling. I sobbed into the toilet as my body quaked with effort, my gut clenching and releasing as if I'd given it some sort of poison it needed to eradicate as quickly as possible. I'd never felt so horrible in my life. I thought the torture would never end. But, after a few minutes of not heaving at all, I sat back against my haunches and wiped at my lips.

Before I felt Bryce stand up.

"What's all this?" he asked.

I fell against the wall, too weak to come up with an excuse.

"Are these... pregnancy tests?" he asked.

All I could do was nod as my eyes fluttered closed.

"Oh, my god," he whispered.

And when I opened my eyes, I expected him to be upset.

I expected him to be upset and worried. I expected him to be angry, or at the very least, disapproving. Tears streamed down my face and neck as I tried to talk. But, every time I opened my mouth, the only thing that happened was hiccups. I was crying and hiccuping, and still feeling sick to my stomach. I couldn't get my legs to function enough to pick me up, and my hands trembled so badly I thought they might dislocate themselves. Then finally, I got some words out.

"I'm so sorry. I-I-I--I didn't know. I--I thought--."

Bryce crouched in front of me. "Sh, sh, sh, sh. Ssshhh, beautiful. It's okay. I'm right here."

"I don't want you to be mad at me. You know I went to get the implant three weeks ago."

"Didn't they do a test before putting it in your arm."

"Yes... but... I think I was too late and--."

He cupped my cheeks and his eyes met mine.

He pulled me up from the floor. "We have to go get that out of you right now. I've read research studies that say that damn thing increases birth defects in fetuses."

My legs caved from beneath me. "What?"

He caught me, then scooped me into his arms. "Doctor. Now. We need that thing out of your arm. "Willow!"

Marie Lee yelled from her room. "Daddy!?"

"Get to the truck, sweetie! We gotta take Willow to the doctor!"

Everything rushed around me, and I just wanted it to stop. Somehow, I ended up in the truck in the front seat with

Marie Lee strapped into her car seat in the back. My head lobbed over just as Bryce jumped up into the driver's seat, cranking the engine as quickly as he could.

But, when I reached my hand out and settled it against his thigh, he paused.

"What's wrong? Are you feeling sick again? Do you need some water before we head out?" he asked.

I furrowed my brow. "You aren't angry."

He blinked. "Why in the world would I be angry?"

"Because I'm--well, I, uh..."

He took my hand in his. "All of those tests were positive, right?"

I nodded slowly. "Yeah."

"And those weren't fake?"

I snickered. "What kind of person do you think I am?"

He grinned. "The most amazing person who's going to make a fantastic mother."

Marie Lee called out from the backseat. "Gotta go! Wiwwow's sickies!"

I smiled. "You're happy about this, aren't you?"

He kissed the back of my hand. "I could think of nothing else more amazing than having a baby with the woman I love."

Marie Lee gasped. "Baby!? Wike me!?"

I sighed. "I love you so much."

Bryce settled my hand back down against his thigh. "I love you, too. But, right now? You need a doctor for multiple reasons."

As he tore out of the driveway, skidding his tires in the process, Marie Lee screamed for joy. Oh, she's a thrill-seeker, all right—possibly even a barrel racer, like her father. I closed my eyes and drew in deep breaths while Bryce called every possible OBGYN in the city, begging them for an open appointment within the next few minutes. And after finding a doctor that could squeeze us in, we rushed halfway across town to get to the office.

An office that just so happened to belong to the best OBGYN in the state.

Everything happened in a blur. I remembered someone greeting me, but I was much too sick to respond. Somehow, I ended up in a room lying down on an unforgiving white bed while hooked up to a heart rate monitor as well as a blood pressure cuff.

And after running their own pregnancy test, the first thing they did was get that implant out of my arm.

Which didn't feel very nice in the process.

"Shit," I hissed.

"Sit! Sit! Sit!" Marie Lee exclaimed.

I shook my head. "No, no, pretty girl. We don't use that word."

Bryce chuckled. "She may or may not have already learned it from me."

I rolled my eyes. "What parents we're going to make."

The doctor giggled. "All right, the implant has been removed, and I've got you a prescription in for some heavy-duty prenatals. Your hCG levels are right where they should be, but your iron levels are really low."

Bryce hopped in. "Is that a bad thing?"

I looked over at the doctor. "Low iron?"

The doctor nodded. "Nothing a prenatal pill with iron in it won't cure. But, I do want to get an ultrasound while you're here. Make sure there's nothing else going on. Is that okay?"

I looked over at Bryce. "Do you want to do that?"

And when I saw the light behind his eyes, I knew we were going to be okay.

"I'd love to have one done," he said.

With Marie Lee on his shoulders and his hand tightly gripping mine, the doctor rolled in an ultrasound machine. She squeezed that cold-ass gel onto my stomach and rubbed it around with the wand before a sound filled the room.

Tha-thump, tha-thump, tha-thump, tha-thump, tha-thump.

I gasped. "Is that...?"

Bryce squeezed my hand. "It is."

Marie Lee giggled. "Tha's my brudder."

I giggled with joy as tears rushed my eyes. "Or sister."

Bryce kissed my forehead. "Whatever it is, it's going to be perfect. And you're going to be a fantastic mother."

I gazed into his upside-down eyes. "I love you so much."

He kissed my lips softly. "I love you, too."

And as I laid there, holding his hand while staring at a monitor projecting our child's heartbeat, I knew we were going to be okay. I knew this was forever. I knew this was where I belonged, forever, and always. By Bryce and Marie

Lee's side. By our child's side. Raising them and helping them and loving them throughout the years.

No matter what might come my way as a member of the Remington family, I was looking forward to a life full of love and adventure on the Rocking R Ranch.

Follow Sadie and Will's story in Cowboy's Sassy Roommate

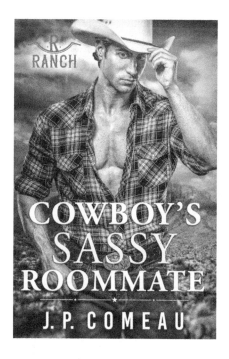

Made in the USA
Monee, IL
30 May 2021